Max saw Blythe v

He slowed, giving himself the pleasure of simply looking at her in the little black dress. No more than a slip, really, and it hugged every curve.

If he closed his eyes, he could remember exactly how the curves had felt in his hands.

He quickened his step, moving silently, and sneaked up behind her. "You're not escaping from me," he whispered into her ear.

Blythe jumped and shivered in his arms. "Go back to the party," she said, sounding panicked. "What if my roommate catches you?"

Max started to tell her exactly how little he cared if Candy caught them, but realized he had a much better use for their few stolen minutes. Gently he turned her toward him and bent his head way, way down to kiss her. She moaned and wrapped her arms around his neck.

The elevator came and he backed her into it. His fingertips were at the hem of her skirt before the doors closed....

Dear Reader,

The words *When the Lights Go Out* once conjured up images of romance, mystery and excitement in my mind. During last August's East Coast blackout, those words took on a whole new meaning. In Manhattan where I live, no lights also meant no stoplights at the intersections, no subways, no trains to the suburbs, packed buses, closed groceries *and* restaurants and no elevators in a city of skyscrapers. Worst of all, there were people in those subways and on those elevators when they ground to a halt.

New York rallied, as it always does. There were unheard-of demonstrations of good manners at those unlighted intersections, and city dwellers invited stranded suburbanites to sleep over. When I discovered my neighbors stuck in the elevator, I'd love to report that I was as levelheaded and resourceful as Blythe Padgett. Alas, my rescue efforts involved a lot of running up and down the stairs while trying to get 911 on the phone, and in between, shouting hysterical words of encouragement down the elevator shaft.

I wonder how many people ended up in the wrong bed like Blythe and found their lives changed forever. That's something we'll never know, because they're not telling. Forgive me, Blythe and Max, for revealing your deep dark secret....

Barbara Daly
bdalybooks@aol.com

Books by Barbara Daly

HARLEQUIN TEMPTATION
859—A LONG HOT CHRISTMAS
887—TOO HOT TO HANDLE
953—MISTLETOE OVER MANHATTAN

BARBARA DALY

WHEN THE LIGHTS GO OUT...

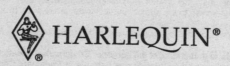

HARLEQUIN®

TORONTO • NEW YORK • LONDON
AMSTERDAM • PARIS • SYDNEY • HAMBURG
STOCKHOLM • ATHENS • TOKYO • MILAN • MADRID
PRAGUE • WARSAW • BUDAPEST • AUCKLAND

To all those friends with whom I shared the August 2003 blackout—to the doormen who stayed on, to my husband, George, and our stranded houseguest Eitan for cheerfully eating tuna salad sandwiches for dinner in the dining capital of the United States.

And especially to my neighbors the Pingitores, who retained their elegance and dignity throughout their long ordeal in the elevator, and to those tireless NYPD officers who rescued them.

ISBN 0-373-69174-2

WHEN THE LIGHTS GO OUT...

Copyright © 2004 by Barbara Daly

www.eHarlequin.com

Printed in U.S.A.

"WHATCHA GOTTA DO IS gut up and frigging go for it."

"Frigging?" Blythe Padgett looked up at her best friend, her roommate, her co-worker, her guardian devil. "Very good, Candy. Last month it was *effing*. You've toned it down another notch."

"Bart's on my case." Candy Jacobsen was a tall, beautiful blonde with a mouth as filthy as the pan the mechanic drained your old oil into. Her passion for expletives was only one of the reasons her news stories invariably needed a rewrite, a task Blythe was performing at this very moment, providing Candy the time and space to interfere in her life.

Not that Candy needed much time to interfere in Blythe's life. Not at any time in the seven years they'd been friends had she ever been too busy to do that.

She didn't need much space, either. The *New York Telegraph* offices occupied three floors of a large, undistinguished building in Times Square. City Desk editor Bart Klemp and his crew of reporters and staff, including Blythe and Candy, occupied the fifth floor, which was basically one enormous high-ceilinged room with scuffed hardwood floors and grandly proportioned, infrequently cleaned windows.

At one time, the office had contained nothing more than rows of desks. The sounds of clacking typewriters and jangling phones must have bounced off the walls and ceiling to create a din loud enough to rattle those big windows. Then someone had come up with the bright idea of separate cubicles. These were nothing more than six-feet-high, square doorless partitions made of a porous synthetic material, but they at least gave the illusion of privacy and cut down on the noise level. When someone else came up with the even brighter idea of computers, and phones were engineered to announce incoming calls by flashing or buzzing softly, the result was the busy hum that prevailed outside the cubicle where Blythe was currently trying to fix Candy's story and Candy was trying to fix Blythe's life.

Obviously undistracted from her cause, Candy slid off the edge of Blythe's desk to pace the tiny cubicle a few steps this way and that on her stiletto heels. "If you don't start strutting your stuff, you're never going to find another—" she came to a halt, then said "—boyfriend."

Blythe knew the term Candy had wanted to use, but couldn't quite bring herself to say "frig-buddy."

"Because," Candy said, pointing a long, frosted-pearl fingernail at Blythe, "until you find another guy, you're not going to get over Thor. You can't spend your life thinking no man will ever want you just because—"

"His name wasn't Thor," Blythe mumbled. "It was Sven."

"Thor, Sven, who cares? Male meat. Problem was that he was so full of steroids he couldn't—"

"Candy!" Blythe vengefully deleted *cataclysmic* and typed in *major*. It reduced the verve of Candy's story nicely. Candy could use a bit of verve reduction.

"So what you have to do," Candy said, "is sleep

with somebody. Anybody. Break through the frigging barrier. Then you'll be okay. Are you about finished with that?"

Candy and Blythe had both landed jobs with the *New York Telegraph* right out of college. A mere three years later, Candy was a hotshot crime reporter with high hopes of getting a job with the venerable *Times*. Blythe was still a proofreader. Bart Klemp, the city desk editor, had declared that "Blythe Padgett's a darned good writer, but she wouldn't know news if she woke up in bed with it."

Everybody seemed determined for her to wake up in bed with...something.

Rewrites were currently the biggest thing going on in her life. This one was Candy's report of a shocking drug bust on a sedate street of town houses in Greenwich Village. As fed up as Blythe felt with the entire world, it was going to read like a story from the Obituaries editor in the cubicle next door when Blythe was finished with it.

"And I've got just the guy for you."

She'd tuned Candy out for a moment, but this statement made her tune swiftly back in. "You what? Who?"

"He grew up next door to me," Candy said, "so we know he's not a strangler or an axe murderer."

"Oh! Wonderful! Those are my *top* qualifications. Have I ever met him?" One of Candy's many kindnesses was to take the orphaned Blythe home for holidays. Candy's family had become her family. In spite of enjoying every privilege money could buy, the Jacobsens were as broken as any family could be and fell just short of being certifiably insane, but any kind of family was better than none.

"Oh, no. His parents moved ages ago," Candy said, "but I kept in touch with him. He's living in Boston now. I don't know...he was always sort of special to me, I guess, like the big brother I never had. He's attractive. And sensitive—for a guy, anyway. I mean, he's a shrink and a shrink has to be sensitive. He was educated to be sensitive. He gets paid big bucks to be sensitive. I know I can trust him to be nice to you. You could have a few dates and let nature take its course."

"What's his—"

"But I have a feeling nature will take its course the second you lay eyes on each other, and he sees what a sexy little hotpot you are."

Candy was pacing in circles now, and gave Blythe's curly red hair an affectionate ruffle on her way around the desk, but Blythe still felt irritated. A hotpot was a menu item in a Mongolian restaurant. How could a hotpot be sexy? Candy was really very careless in her use of language. "Candy, come on!" Blythe said, deleting a string of flamboyant adjectives from the news story. "I don't know anything about this old friend of yours. I might not like him at all."

"You don't have to like him. You just have to have sex with him." Candy fanned herself with a galley proof from the stack on Blythe's desk. Midafternoon, mid-August, New York—these three factors were more than the air-conditioning in the prewar building that housed the *Telegraph* offices could handle.

"No way I'd go to bed with a total stranger," Blythe said firmly. "Certainly not with a man I didn't like."

But Candy's face had taken on a dangerously dreamy expression. "That's how I lost my virginity," she said. "I kept saving it and saving it, because my mother said I should save myself for the right man."

It sounded comfortably motherly, but Candy's mother still seemed to be looking for the right man—and having gone through three husbands in the search, the evidence pointed strongly toward the likelihood that she hadn't been saving herself.

"But there never was the right man," Candy went on like a voice-over to Blythe's thoughts, "and I saw myself getting older and older without finding him. One day I said, 'You've got to start somewhere.' So I went straight for the quarterback, not a total stranger, but let's just say we'd never talked. I'm not sure he knew how to."

Wellesley, where the two of them had gone to college, Blythe on a National Merit scholarship, was still a women's college and didn't have a football team. "How old were you?" Blythe asked, changing "biggest haul of the decade" to "confiscation of a large amount of product."

"Fifteen."

"Fifteen! No wonder you panicked!" Blythe removed one last random comma from Candy's story and sent the file to the printer. "I bet you're sorry now that you settled for the high school quarterback."

"Sorry? Honey, it made me what I am today, as sexually healthy as the horse that man was hung like. Whoo. I still get wet just thinking about him." She licked her lips.

Blythe tried not to pinch *her* lips together. "Well, thanks for telling me about your friend. What did you say his name—"

"I told him about you, too."

"Candy, you can't do that!"

"I can and did." Candy looked too smug.

"What exactly did you do?" Thinking of the myriad

possibilities, the limitless nature of Candy's imagination, made Blythe intensely nervous.

"Told him you and he should get together. And guess what? He's coming to New York for a conference."

"When?"

"Today."

"How nice. I'm sure the conference will keep him very busy. But maybe sometime in the distant future..."

"Tonight," Candy said.

"*What?*"

"Tonight. You have a date with him tonight. Seven o'clock. I'm going to tell my date to meet me here, give you two some frigging—"

Blythe levitated out of her chair and ripped the last page out of the printer so fast the ink trailed down into the margin. "That's it," she said. "Now you've gone too far."

"Thanks," Candy said, grabbing the pages out of Blythe's hands. "Face it, Blythe, you needed a push."

"A push, maybe! Not my sad story laid before a total stranger! Not a date with a man who assumes I'm desperate to jump in the sack with him!" She held out her hands in supplication. "We should meet for lunch first, no, coffee first, then lunch. No, talk on the phone first, then coffee, then lunch. We should have e-mailed before he even called me on the phone."

"Blythe, Blythe..." Candy shook her head. "You're too frigging conservative."

"I must have been born that way. It sure wasn't parental influence," Blythe said stubbornly, plunking herself back down in her chair. Her parents had died in an automobile accident before they'd had a chance to influence her one way or the other. Although losing them had had a profound influence on what she wanted out of her own life.

"I know, I know," Candy said, heaving a dramatic sigh of resignation. "Okay, we'll do it your way. I'll call him and tell him to ask you out for coffee tomorrow instead. Hope I can reach him." She glanced at her watch, and her inch-long nails glittered as she moved them around in the fluorescent light of the newsroom. "God a'mighty. I gotta get outta here and cover a take-down in the Bronx."

As Candy took off at warp speed, Blythe took note of her working clothes—a shrunken-looking cream T-shirt, a natural linen skirt too short to bend over in and a pair of bone-colored, spike-heeled pumps that came to a sharp point well beyond her toes. She resembled a rope of taffy. Blythe chased her to the door of the newsroom. "You sure you want to take the subway up to the Bronx in that outfit?"

Candy paused long enough to look down at herself. "Think I should take a cab? Nope, takes too long."

She took off again. Blythe gazed after her for a moment, then went slowly back to her desk. *As sexually healthy as the horse that man was hung like. As sexually healthy as the horse like which that man was hung.*

She blew a nasty-sounding raspberry at the computer. Candy interfered because she cared about her. Blythe knew this, would never forget how Candy had become her champion the moment Blythe entered the freshman class at Wellesley with absolutely nothing going for her but her brains. She didn't know why she'd awakened Candy's sympathy, but under Candy's wing Blythe had blossomed—at least, as much as she was ever going to blossom. She'd made friends, joined clubs, learned to girl-talk, learned to laugh. Still, at times she wished Candy would back off and let her be miserable. This was one of those times.

Resigned, she picked up a stack of galleys and focused her gaze on them. Suddenly, with a flash of monitors going black as computers shut down and the grinding sound of air-conditioning coming to a halt, the world dimmed.

From her cubicle Blythe could hear the newsroom catapulting into chaos. "What the hell?" somebody shouted.

"I've lost my story!" came from the Obituaries editor next door.

Blythe got up and darted around the corner to comfort him. "In a minute the generator will kick in," she assured the hysterical young man who was still staring at his screen and jabbing at the enter key as if that would bring back his golden prose. "You won't lose the whole story."

Everyone else in the newsroom seemed to have gotten up at once. Reporters and editors were milling around like a herd of sheep, consulting each other, wringing hands or trying to act blasé. Someone began raising the blinds they'd closed earlier against the searing sunshine, and the omnipresent dust of Manhattan swirled in the harsh rays.

One by one the staffers picked up their phones to find them dead, then stabbed at the keys of their cell phones, only to slam them down in frustration.

Silence fell just as suddenly as the chaos had erupted when their shepherd, Bart Klemp, plodded out from his office at the end of the room, a private office with a door and actual walls that went all the way to the ceiling.

Blythe was reminded of movies in which the benevolent plant-eating brontosaurus moved across the landscape, making the earth tremble with each ponderous step. This was a very odd comparison because Bart wasn't a particularly tall man and he was chunky rather than obese. It was something in his attitude. Bart always looked as if he and his entire species were about to go extinct, and the thought made him terribly sad.

"I've been listening to the radio," he said, "and the power's out."

We know that much without listening to a radio.

Bart's face turned scarlet. Everybody must have been giving him the same "Duh!" look Blythe probably had on her face. "What I mean is," Bart said, "that it's not just us. It's the power grid that serves the whole East Coast, Toronto south to Maryland and west into Michigan."

The buzz in the newsroom was like a crowd-noise sound effect on an old radio show.

"Here on the home front, the generator's not working, either, and the phone system's down—they need electricity from somewhere, apparently. Anybody wants a briefing in electrical engineering, don't look at me. All I know is nothing's working at the *Telegraph*, and those of you still putting stories together, you're going to have a hard time getting a circuit on your cell phones."

Blythe still didn't have a cell phone, and while she reflected that it really was well past time to be the last on the block to get one, Bart paused to rest a beefy hand on a desk and go even more fully into collapse mode. "I don't know who's going to show up from the night crew, so I'd appreciate it if some of you guys would stick around, see what we can pull together for a paper tomorrow afternoon if we get the power back in time. We've got radios to get the news, find out if it's a terrorist attack or a lightning strike or somebody just screwed up, so there's no excuse for us not to have those stories ready to print just as fast as the *Times* will."

Blythe had her hand halfway up in the air. This was a dream come true—not that she was happy the entire East Coast had to suffer on behalf of one of her dreams—but this was her chance. Help get the paper out under impossible conditions. Save the day. Be a hero. Be indispensable.

But Bart wasn't asking for volunteers. He was reading off a list of names. Hers wasn't on it.

There it was, in actions that spoke louder than words. She wasn't indispensable. Not that she didn't know she wasn't indispensable to the *Telegraph*, but it still hurt to have it confirmed. Gone, gone were her dreams of spending a few years being a latter-day Lois Lane, dashing about the city to uncover the facts for a front page story, always on a tight deadline while the entire newsroom waited with bated breath for her return, because if she didn't get the story, the *Telegraph* would die a humiliating death in bankruptcy and all would be lost.

That part of the dream she'd have to revise to suit the power outage, but the second part remained intact. That at the end of an endless day, victorious, having saved the paper, she'd go home to her own personal superhero.

Crumpling inside, she turned toward her cubicle to get her handbag. In the background, she heard the political editor ask Bart, "When was our new guy supposed to land? I was counting on him to get out the columns on this City Council scandal..."

Counting on him. When would anybody ever count on her?

Feeling useless and defeated, Blythe walked down the four flights of stairs and onto the street. The subway system wasn't working obviously, but the buses were. Perhaps a hundred people were waiting at the first bus stop. Twenty minutes later, after several already-stuffed buses had passed them by, flashing the Wait for Next Bus sign, she decided to splurge on a taxi and moved to the middle of the block to flag one down. Fifteen minutes worth of already-occupied taxis later, she knew walking was her only option.

Walking was dangerous. It gave her time to think.

Her stomach lurched with worry. Poor Candy. Was she all right? Was she one of the terrified people stuck on subway trains in the dark and the heat? How would she ever get home? Candy's poor friend, the shrink. Blythe hadn't even wrung his name out of Candy, and now she might never meet him.

What was he like, Candy's friend? You'd expect Candy's friends to be dingbats, but the ones Blythe had met on those holiday visits had been quite nice people, Candy being the wild child among them. So he probably *was* nice. And sensitive.

If she'd let Candy have her own way and the power hadn't gone out and her friend *had* arrived for his blind therapy session with Blythe—you could hardly call it a date—she would have handled it in *her* own way. She would have offered him a drink and explained to him that, as fond as they both were of Candy, he ought to know that his friend had grown up to be a nutcase, an instant-gratification freak, a steamroller with no brakes.

Well, no, it wouldn't do to criticize an old friend. She'd put the blame on herself instead.

"I'm delighted to meet you, of course," she would have said, "but Candy overreacted to my little, ah, problem. You mustn't feel any obligation to take me out." *And don't even think about taking me to bed.*

And he might have said, "Ha, ha. Candy overreact? You must be joking." And they might have had a good laugh together and maybe met for coffee sometime.

But this pleasant little exchange wasn't likely to happen. Blythe didn't like thinking about what might have happened to Candy's friend.

His plane might be speeding desperately toward an airport where the air traffic controllers had electricity and the runway had lights, knowing the gas gauge was sinking lower, lower, lower. He'd feel the plane begin to lose altitude and think regretfully of the wild affair he might have had with Candy's little redheaded roommate, a spitfire, a hot-blooded sex goddess, cursing fate for what he'd missed out on.

Blythe took in a sharp breath. He might have crashed while he was cursing fate.

Now he'd never know the truth, that the only thing hot about her was her hair color. That and her passion for correct spelling and good grammar.

Or he might still be at Logan Airport, simply cursing because his flight had been canceled. Wherever he was, she felt he must be cursing. How could he have grown up next door to Candy without being a world-class composer of creative expletives?

Blythe stopped daydreaming long enough to take stock of where she was. She'd almost done the crosstown part of her journey home. Now for the uptown part. She'd keep walking while she watched for a bus

or a taxi. *Just* thirty-five blocks. Thirty-five blocks was
nothing more than a good morning walk. Good afternoon walk. What time was it, anyway? Her watchband
had slid around on her sweaty wrist, and she scooted it
back. It was nearly six. Okay, thirty-five blocks was a
good evening constitutional.

She had plenty of company. The sidewalks were
packed in midtown, then thinned out as she moved up
Madison Avenue into the East Sixties, where limousine
drivers were delivering their wealthy employers home
to their town houses. The heat and humidity weighed
her down, so she paused occasionally for rest and win-
dow-shopping at stores that were closed down, had
probably closed immediately after the blackout for security reasons, or to give their owners and managers a
slight chance of making it home. Sweating in her flowered skirt and coral T-shirt, shopping didn't grab her
attention.

She ought to look for another job, go somewhere she
could feel successful, but she was scared to confront a
break in her steady salary and benefits. She was alone
in the big city.

She was alone in the big world was what she was. Or
would be, if it weren't for Candy.

If she got any more maudlin, she'd sound like a character in a soap opera. She'd be okay. She could take
care of herself. She'd worked hard. That scholarship
had given her an excellent education. She just hadn't
found the right job yet, that was all.

Her smile faded as she had a fleeting vision of herself in jeans and a sweatshirt, loading a host of bright-
eyed children into a station wagon in the driveway of a
spotless, warm and cheery white clapboard house in
the suburbs that still smelled of the bacon and eggs

she'd cooked for breakfast, the tuna fish sandwiches she'd lovingly packed in their lunch boxes along with rosy apples and bags of chips. This was her other dream, a dream far more important than the Lois-Lane-saves-the-paper dream.

What she really wanted was to be a wife and mother. In her spare time she might write a weekly column in the local newspaper, something on housekeeping. Or parenting. She'd volunteer at her kids' school, of course, and might even run for City Council in a quiet little suburb in Connecticut or New Jersey where the major issues were fence height and lawn maintenance. She'd keep her brain active, but the children—and her superhero—would come first.

This was a secret she kept in her heart. She didn't have a single friend, especially not Candy, who would understand. The aggressive, career-oriented women of Manhattan would view homemaking as a nightmare. To Blythe, who'd never had a home and family, it sounded like heaven on earth.

Unfortunately the scene needed a handsome, loving, sexy man to kiss goodbye while the kids piled into the car, a man who could understand and support her dream and even express his love for her and the children by boiling the eggs for the tuna fish salad. She'd find that man someday. Just not quite yet.

At long last, she stepped gratefully into the lobby of the building where she and Candy shared an apartment, expecting the relief of a delicious blast of air-conditioning when, of course, there wasn't any.

Santiago, the day doorman, was still on the job. "Miss Padgett." He sounded relieved. "You made it home."

"Just barely," she croaked. "All I want is a nice long shower—we do have water, don't we?"

An uneasy look came over his face. "We have water." He cleared his throat. "Not necessarily hot water, but water. What we don't have is elevators."

She and Candy lived on the twenty-third floor. "I thought the elevators had an emergency backup system."

He shuffled his feet. "It's not working. Guess it has to get electricity from somewhere."

She'd already heard this from Bart. "I know," she said kindly. "If I want a lesson in electrical engineering, I'll have to get it from somebody else. Okay, so I'll walk up."

"It's dark, and I mean dark, in the stairwells," Santiago went on. "I bought all the flashlights the hardware store down the street had left. Take one. First come, first served. I'd walk up with you, but J.R. and I are the only staff here. We stayed on because the night shift didn't make it in."

She took a moment to send out hugs to people stranded on subways, stuck in elevators, hoping Candy wasn't among them. "Have they closed the bridges and tunnels?"

Santiago nodded. "Eddie called in," he said. "He can't get out of Brooklyn."

That definitely took care of her date-under-duress. "I knew we'd live to regret the age of technology," Blythe said as she headed for the stairs that spiraled up through the building and ended closest to hers and Candy's apartment. She opened the door and almost lost heart. With no windows in the stairwell, no light reached it at all. But it was the only way home. Grasp-

ing her flashlight, she aimed it up into the darkness
and got her feet moving.

Second floor, third, fourth, fifth...

She'd never buy a StairMaster. Who needed one, as
undependable as New York was.

Sixth, seventh, eighth...

When she'd trapped a wonderful husband and delivered numerous adorable children to worry about,
she'd be grateful she'd opted for that house in suburbia. Two floors, three, max. She could hear some noise
going on above her. It was comforting, knowing other
people were in the building. She wouldn't have that in
suburbia, but then she wouldn't be climbing twenty-
two flights of dark stairs, either.

Ninth, tenth, eleventh...

The higher she climbed, the worse she felt about
Candy's friend. Now, thinking of him in a state of crisis, or worse, she wished she'd been more receptive to
Candy's idea, had let him take her into his arms, kiss
her, let nature take its course, just as Candy had assured her it would.

At least pestered Candy for his "frigging" name!

She frowned. The heat and isolation were getting to
her. She hadn't done anything bad to Candy's friend
yet. She couldn't have taken him into her arms and let
nature take its course because he hadn't gotten there.
She still had time to make things right. Feeling she'd
had a narrow escape from a level of guilt she'd never
get over, she collapsed on the first step leading up to
the twelfth floor, drew her knees up, rested her forehead on them and closed her eyes, reflecting on the
true value of certain New York status symbols, the Upper East Side apartment, the higher floor.

The noise from above had increased in volume. She

suddenly realized that what she was hearing was not the voices of neighbors but frantic pounding and shouting. It galvanized her into action. She could feel her hair standing on end. Someone was being attacked, maybe killed! What manners, to mug somebody during a crisis! And in such a nice, safe building! Was there no honor among thieves anymore?

She had a whistle and a can of Mace she'd carried around in her handbag for two years without needing them. She hoped they still worked. Where was the shouting coming from? She hated to retrace a single precious step. She'd start on the twelfth floor. Dredging up one last burst of energy, she raced up the steps and encountered a locked door.

Locked for security reasons, of course. She was pretty sure one of the keys she'd been issued when she and Candy moved in unlocked the stairwell doors. As the pounding intensified and the shouts grew louder, she searched the depths of her handbag for the ring of keys, found them and began jabbing them at the keyhole one at a time. At least the guy was still fighting off the mugger. A key fit, turned and she barreled out into the twelfth-floor hallway, shining her flashlight to the left and to the right, yelling, "Hands up! I've got you covered!"

The shouting stopped. The hall was silent. Nobody was being mugged that she could see. "Hello?" she said timidly. "Is somebody up here."

"Yes."

The voice came from right behind her and several feet above her. Blythe screamed. The flashlight flew out of her hands and the hallway plunged into total darkness.

2

"WHO SAID THAT? Where are you?" On her hands and knees, Blythe scrambled blindly for the flashlight. Her hand closed on it and she clutched it gratefully to her bosom, then remembered why she loved it so much and turned it back on.

"I'm in the elevator. Where did you think I was?"

She shone the light on the bank of elevators. "Which one?" she said. Her voice was shaking. She pounded on the first doors. "In here?" The second. It sent back a hollow sound. "Here?"

She was moving on to the third when she heard, "Stop, damn it. I'm right here in the middle."

She stepped back. "Are you okay?"

There was a silence, then, "No, I'm not okay. I'm stuck in the elevator."

"Besides that," Blythe said.

"That's enough," he said.

"How long have you been in there?"

"Since the lights went out! Can we end the quiz? Is there a way to get out of here?"

She was calming down because she knew the answer to this one. "Yes," she said, speaking slowly as if he were a child. "You pick up the emergency phone and say—"

"It's not working. Neither are the lights. It's really, really dark in here."

Nothing is working, Bart had said. She was beginning to grasp the idea. "We've had a major power outage," she said, "but we'll get you out of there. Don't you worry. Dial 9-1-1. Do you have a cell phone? Because I don't."

"I can't get a signal."

"I'll go back downstairs," she said at last, groaning at the very thought, "and see if J.R. or Santiago has something to pry open the doors."

"No. Don't leave."

She paused. The man was admitting he was frightened. Claustrophobic, maybe. Or just a man trapped for hours in an inky-black box with no connection to the outside world until she'd come. He needed her. Some strong, unidentifiable feeling surged up in her heart. He actually needed her. She couldn't let him down. "Okay, I won't. Maybe I have something in my bag."

"Can you see anything?"

"I have a flashlight."

"Oh. A flashlight. I'd kill for a flashlight."

Poor guy. She aimed the light at the doors. "Can you see this?"

"What?"

"A ray of light."

"No."

Some quality of his voice made her dump the contents of her handbag out on the hall carpet and aim the flashlight at the pile. She had a nail file. Still on the floor, she thrust it through the opening in the doors and wiggled it. "Can you see my nail file?"

"I can't see anything."

"Well, can you feel it?"

"Aim it higher. You sound like you're way below me. The elevator must have stopped between floors."

She stood and reached as high as she could to wiggle the file in.

"There it is!" He sounded like Columbus spotting land. She felt a tug on the file. "It's not going to move the doors, though. Got anything bigger? Wait a minute. I've got a Swiss Army knife."

"You have a knife?"

A spurt of air, something like a snort, came from above her head. "Everybody has a Swiss Army knife. Chill, okay? The knife doesn't belong in the lead paragraph."

It was an odd coincidence that he'd used a journalistic term—lead paragraph. "Okay. Sorry." She reached for the nail file and found that a tiny sharp point had emerged from inside the elevator. "Now we've got two things through."

"More, more."

Blythe was staring down at her comb. It was plastic with a thick, solid handle and long wide-spaced teeth, the kind called an Afro-comb, the only thing Blythe could get through her hair when she'd been out on a windy day. It might work. She grabbed it and began forcing it through the practically nonexistent opening. One tooth took hold. Dizzy with excitement, she pushed harder.

"Ouch."

She stopped pushing. "What happened?"

"Something hit me in the nose. I crouched down here to see if any air was coming through the doors, and..."

"This is good news," Blythe assured him. "It's my

comb. Try to grab it and help me get it through." She instantly felt a tug.

"I've got a grip on it. If I can just bend it without breaking it..."

With a clatter, the nail file and the knife fell from the widening crack in the door through which two sets of long, strong-looking fingers were emerging.

"It's opening!"

"Forget the comb. Help me push the doors."

Blythe tucked the flashlight into her waistband. Moving closer for leverage, she put her fingertips through the opening and pushed with all her might. Her toe connected with something, the file or the knife, and kicked it through the space below the elevator car. For a moment she froze, listening as it fell down, down, endlessly down the elevator shaft to the basement thirteen floors below. She thought she might faint just waiting for it to hit bottom.

"Keep pushing." He sounded desperate.

"We have a slight problem," she said, willing her voice not to tremble. "You're pretty far up from the floor, actually. If I keep pushing and the doors suddenly open, I'm going to fall down the elevator shaft. Not that anybody would miss me particularly, but I would hate the fall itself, if you know what I..."

"Stop pushing." It was an order. "Let me think." While he thought, a shoulder emerged through the opening above her. "Okay, you step back and pull on the left side—"

"My left or your left?" She was still poised in the middle, one hand on each side of the opening, prepared to die.

"Your left. And I'll push the door to your right. Got it?"

She already had both hands gripped on one door, tugging. "Got it."

"We're almost there, almost there, don't give up."

With a terrifying suddenness, the doors popped open. Blythe fell backward. A suitcase landed on her left knee, followed by a body swinging a smaller bag. It felt like a huge body, a huge, trembling body. It covered her completely. Crisp hair brushed her face.

For a moment he just panted, then he said, "I think I love you. Will you marry me?"

Panic and all, she felt a smile rising to her face. "Let's hold off on total commitment until morning, shall we?" she said.

"You're right." He puffed out the words, still not rolling away from her. "I was being impulsive. Names first. I'm Max. Max Laughton. And actually, I already have a date tonight. Have to meet my obligations first. Unless," he added, sounding hopeful, Blythe thought, "she didn't make it home."

"What floor does your date live on?"

"Twenty-third. I just got into town and it's a blind date, kind of a crazy situation... What's wrong?"

The darkness, the fear, the tension, the relief had finally gotten to Blythe completely. She was shuddering beneath him, and gasped the words out between hysterical giggles.

"I'm your date," she gurgled. "Hi. Welcome to New York."

"YOU OKAY?" MAX ASKED the little person struggling along beside him when they'd reached the fifteenth-floor landing. "Want a rest? You must be worn out. Did you have to walk all the way home from the *Telegraph*?"

"Um-m," was all she said, or moaned, from a spot that just about reached his shoulder. She wasn't what he'd expected. From the sultry, purring voice on the phone that had asked him out for a night on the town as soon as he got to New York, he'd expected her to be more substantial, a blond bombshell, openly and deliberately provocative. Her voice had been full of heat and promise. When he'd quizzed Bart about her—Bart being a longtime friend of his parents and an uncle figure to him—all Bart had said was, "Candy Jacobsen? It'll be quite a welcome."

Max didn't need any light to know that this woman was small, with fluffy hair that looked as if it might be red. She was sexy all right, but didn't act as if she knew she was sexy.

Of course, people often presented a different picture of themselves on the phone. Whatever she was, she'd saved his life and that made her okay with him. More than okay. A person whose feet he'd like to kiss.

"Why...did you come...so early?" she panted.

"I was supposed to come as soon as I got to town."

"Not...seven o'clock?"

"No." He paused and aimed the flashlight at his watch. "Even if I misunderstood, it's after eight now."

"How time flies."

It was merely a whisper. "Not in an elevator, it doesn't," he said, glancing down at the top of her head. They'd reached the seventeenth floor, and she already sounded completely winded. Her shoulders, narrow little shoulders in some kind of a T-shirt, were bent over as she focused on the lighted steps, probably counting them. She must be exhausted, had probably been exhausted the whole time she was rescuing him.

His heart swelled with compassion and something

else—budding heroism. Yes, it was time for him to show the stuff he was made of. Time to be a macho man.

"You're pooped," he said by way of launching his plan.

"I'm fine," she gasped.

"No, you're not. Wait a second." He shouldered his briefcase, grabbed her handbag over her squeak of protest and slung it over his other shoulder, then handed her his larger bag and swept her up into his arms.

"Save your strength," she cried, and began to wriggle.

"You're not helping," he said. She might be little, but hanging on to, say, a hundred-pound wriggling tuna, who was dangling a thirty-pound suitcase way too close to the family jewels, had never been one of his life's goals. "Besides," he groaned, unable to help himself, "what am I saving it for?"

"Later?" she said and looked up at him, pointing the flashlight directly at their faces. She wore an oddly quizzical look. Maybe she *had* had "quite a welcome" planned for him. His body responded to this idea, but he told it to calm down. He needed the blood equally distributed through his veins to make it up the last six flights of stairs.

When he dumped her just inside the stairwell door so she could fumble through her handbag for the key, his knees were trembling in a way that was hardly heroic. He hoped she didn't notice how he staggered behind her down the dark hallway to her door. He'd hoped that when she opened it, the last rays of sunlight would come flooding through her apartment windows, but the room was in shadows. Once he made it inside, he knew he was washed up.

"That was so sweet of you," she was saying, "to carry me the rest of the way. I'm all rested, and you have to be dead on your feet. Sit down, for heaven's sake. I have to get out the candles first, but then would you like a drink?" Her voice faded. Drawers opened and closed. "Water, definitely, but I imagine you could use something stronger. I sure could. We have a pretty good selection. What's your pleasure?"

He'd made it to a sofa he'd spotted in her flashlight beam, where he collapsed facedown with the word, "Scotch," on his lips. It might be the last word he ever uttered. How ignominious.

BEARING A LIGHTED CANDLE, Blythe crept toward the sofa. When he was in range of the light, she simply had to stare at him for a while, at his broad shoulders in a black polo shirt, a tapered back, a narrow waist and a butt to die for—firm, contoured and thoroughly male. His long legs were encased in black jeans, his thigh muscles bulging against the fabric.

His thighs. She was going all tight just thinking about them wrapped around her. This idea of Candy's hadn't been such a bad one after all.

"How do you like your Scotch?" It came out like a moan.

It took him a long time to answer, and when he did, his words sounded as if they were smothered by goose down, which, in fact, they were. "Rocks."

Candle in hand, Blythe scurried to the freezer, automatically pressed a glass to the ice-maker button and remembered nothing was working. She stuck her hand in the storage bin and pulled out slick, already melting cubes.

She was going to make it all up to him. No more

guilt. Even though this was Candy's idea, not hers, he'd gone through hell to get to her and she'd make sure he wasn't sorry. She already knew she wouldn't be. Any man who'd carry her up six flights of stairs had to be as sensitive as Candy had promised.

Forgetful, maybe. She was sure Candy had said he was coming at seven o'clock, and for him to get stuck in the elevator, it meant he'd arrived around four o'clock. But then, Candy was often careless about details.

The important thing was that he was here. They'd have a drink together, she'd give him a chance to rest and come up refreshed, and then they'd see what course nature took.

Who was she kidding? One look at his back and she was ready to go at it like bunnies. For mental health reasons only, of course. When she got a look at his front, she might become uncontrollably aggressive about getting this therapy.

Blythe paused on her way out of the kitchen. If he wanted to. If he found her desirable. That was still the big if. Even a sensitive man had to feel something before he could—well, *could.*

She put the tray of drinks on the coffee table and sat down on the floor right beside his face, or where his face would be if he ever came up for air, moving the candle as close to that spot as she could without setting her eyelashes on fire.

She gulped her water and gazed at him. Gosh, he had a beautiful profile. His hair was the very dark brown of good chocolate, the seventy percent kind, and his skin was a warm tan. She'd have to wait to see the eyes under those long dark lashes. They were probably brown. She had a preference for blue eyes, but she wasn't going to cross him off on the basis of one little failure to meet specifications.

The distinctive scent of the Scotch seemed to rouse him. His head rolled toward her until at last she got the full impact of his strong, regular features—his straight, narrow nose and a mouth with a full, curved lower lip. Blythe felt her tongue curl in anticipation, and at that moment, his closest eye opened and squinted against the candlelight.

Miracle of miracles, his eyes were blue, a deep, dark, magnificent blue. At least one of them was. In due course, Blythe was sure she'd get a glimpse of the other one.

The closest eyebrow quirked up. "After all we've been through," he said, sounding less breathless, "why do you look so surprised to see me? I mean, you made an offer, and under the circumstances, I'm damned glad I accepted."

With a snap, Blythe brought her lower lip up to meet her upper one. The way he put it wasn't quite the way it had happened. Candy had made the offer, but why quibble over details? Dear Candy, wise beyond her years, had been right. It was time to get over Thor—no, Sven—and the man to get her over Sven was lying right here in front of her, much too tired to be sent back down the stairs. He was trapped. She'd caught herself a live one.

Odd that Candy had called him "attractive," not "the sexiest man alive," and that she hadn't mentioned his luscious baritone voice, which was making Blythe's spinal column vibrate. But now that she'd met him, she realized it didn't matter what his voice sounded like. When you had a body like that, a voice like his was just frosting on the beefcake.

The real question was: How had Candy let this one get away? More than that, why was she simply handing him over to Blythe? Now that was what you called a good friend.

Blythe smiled and moved a little closer. "I wasn't actually expecting you to show up," she admitted, feeling like a cartoon character with stars on springs popping out of her eyes. "Most men would have stood a woman up in these circumstances. Of course, there weren't any circumstances when you got here."

"I still would have shown up. I'm always at the right place at the right time. Rain, snow, sleet, hail, just like the postman. It's part of my job."

"I'm glad to hear it. Dependability is crucial in your profession." She'd heard that people fell apart when their shrinks went on vacation. She wondered if he saw patients on Saturdays and Sundays. Maybe he could come to New York on weekends, or she could go to Boston.

Whoa. She was getting way ahead of herself. It was more likely that this would be a one-night stand, or rather a single therapy session to help her get over the disastrous effect Sven had had on her.

Maybe this sort of therapy was his specialty, which he used on all his female patients. An unexpected, uncalled-for bolt of jealousy made her scalp prickle.

"Take a sip of Scotch," she said encouragingly. Time was passing. Since he seemed to have difficulty moving his head, she added, "Want a straw?" She held the candle even closer to his face, hoping she didn't look too much like a witch trying to intimidate an agent of Satan, because he didn't look at all like an agent of Satan, nor did she have any desire to intimidate him. Seduce him? That was something else altogether.

"No." Two perfectly matched dark blue eyes glared at her as he righted himself on the sofa and reached for the glass. He downed it in one desperate gulp. "That's the first liquid I've had since noon," he said.

Blythe dashed for the kitchen to refill the glass. "How terrible. Here. Drink some more." She sat down beside him on the sofa and watched him closely as he drank.

He took one sip, and his glare faded into a warm, soft glow. "Much better," he said, leaning against the cushions. "I'll be back to normal in a minute."

"Good," Blythe said. "As soon as you've revived, let's get right to it."

"Excuse me?"

Her face heated up. "That is, if you want to now that you've met me."

He sat up a little straighter. "Sure I want to. But I don't think we can get right *to* anywhere right now."

"Oh, I didn't mean you should take me to dinner," Blythe assured him. "Just to bed."

She felt the jolt of his body in the shoulder that brushed against hers. He whipped around to stare at her, his eyes wide. His drink slipped out of his hand and landed in his lap.

Blythe shrieked.

He leaped up, shaking his jeans loose from his crotch, while ice cubes hit the coffee table and the floor with a clatter.

"I'm so sorry," Blythe cried. "What did I say that upset you?" She fumbled her way into the kitchen and took a stack of dish towels out of a drawer. She really didn't need to ask. Now that he'd met her, he wasn't interested in going to bed with her. She followed the candlelight back into the living room and clapped the towels against his wet trousers. A sound curled up from his throat, something between, *"aargh"* and *"aiiiee,"* followed by a muttered, "I'll take care of it, thanks."

Realizing she was hanging on to a rather personal part of him, Blythe let him take over the towels and backed away, feeling even more miserable, inept and undesirable. Her shoulders slumped. "You don't want to go to bed with me, right?"

"Wrong."

"It's okay. I understand. Nobody... What did you say?"

Silently he mopped at his trousers for another moment, then dropped the towels on the coffee table. Turning to her, he curled his hands around her shoulders. His eyes sparked in the dim light as he gazed down at her and said, "I can't think of anything I'd rather do than make love with you."

MAX HAD A STRONG FEELING he was missing a link in the conversational chain, but he was in no mood to go looking for it. Not accept a gift handed to him by the power outage, fate itself? Not want to go to bed with a small, artistically rounded, redheaded, freckled—

Because now, in the candlelight, he could see her just fine, and she was the most huggable woman he'd ever imagined making love to. Her hair was, in fact, red, curly and out of control. He wondered if that faint smattering of freckles covered her whole body. His brain responded to the vision, sending a jet of sudden desire straight to his crotch.

Yes, he'd be happy to go to bed with her. More than happy. Enthusiastic.

Under certain conditions.

"Really?" she said to him, breaking into his thoughts. "You really want to go to bed with me? You're not just saying what you think you're supposed to say?" She wore the most hopeful expression he'd ever seen on a human being.

It was a weird conversation, especially coming from a woman who'd sounded confident to the point of being a ballbuster on the telephone, but that hopeful expression got to him. "Really," he assured her. "Couldn't be more real. A totally genuine feeling. One with visible physical symptoms." He'd probably gone far enough in that direction with someone he barely knew. "But I thought—well, I thought we'd spend a little time getting acquainted first."

He had to throw that in. The voice of his conscience was nagging relentlessly at him. He knew the pitfalls of sleeping with a co-worker, of mixing business with pleasure, plus in this case, he had to make sure she was sane and capable of making judgment calls before he rushed her off to bed. "You know. The old who, what, when, where and why." He smiled, making the point that they were both journalists, the only thing they had in common as far as he knew. "You tell me about your job and your family, the dog you had growing up, then I tell you about..."

"I can see how a person in your profession would feel that way," she said to the underside of his chin. Her voice sounded soft and breathless, but not in the least suggestive, and the words tumbled out. Even more amazingly, her hands, light and deft, fluttered back and forth along his arms in a way that was effectively punching his conscience in the gut. "But I didn't have a dog, and I do have a serious need to rush. The time is at hand. I need to get it over with before I lose my nerve. Unless, of course, you're too tired."

He'd never felt less tired in his life. This was the kind of situation a teenage kid dreamed about finding himself in, but Max wasn't a teenage kid anymore. He knew in his heart she was reacting to fatigue, fear and uncertainty. He'd heard that people caught in life-and-death situations had sex with each other when they wouldn't otherwise have thought of doing anything so impulsive. Maybe the power outage was having the same effect on her. He tilted her face up to give it another once-over. Her skin felt like cream to the touch. This close, in the light of the flickering candles, he could see that her eyes were green, a light, bright green, the color of new leaves in the spring. She was a little tense, a little nervous, but she seemed sane enough.

His heart rate sped up. "People are so different in person," he said hoarsely and with difficulty. "That phone call left me thinking you were a lady with plenty of nerve." He replayed the "welcome you to New York" call in his head and tried to relate it to the woman who was currently turning his temperature up to Broil. But he didn't try very hard because that had been a phone call, and this woman was a tangible, embraceable fact.

Or he'd asphyxiated in the elevator and had gone to heaven. Either one was fine with him.

"Forget the phone call," she said with a sigh that tickled his throat. "You shouldn't believe anything you hear in that kind of phone call. The truth is, I barely have enough nerve to cross the street on a Don't Walk sign." Her eyes shifted away. "Can we just do it?" she asked him. "Fast?"

He'd done his best to behave responsibly, but he wasn't campaigning for sainthood. This time when he swept her up into his arms, she felt as light as cotton candy. Her tiny squeal only intensified the suddenly purposeful sensations thudding through his body. "Yes and no," he said, carrying her toward the promising-looking door ahead of him.

"The other way," she said, trying to whirl him back around behind the sofa. "What do you mean, yes and no?"

Keeping a tight grip on her, he changed direction, shoved a door open, gratefully observed a sea of white that showed up even in the near-darkness and laid her down on it.

"Yes, we can do it. Just not fast." Sinking down beside her, he moved his mouth across hers tentatively, no more than brushing her lips, seeking their shape and form. They were full, firm, warm, sweet—and already opening to his touch.

The kiss knifed into him so deeply he wanted to groan, but he couldn't. She'd seized him too tightly, her hands working his nape and her mouth seeking his with unmistakable hunger.

That did it. He told his conscience to take note of the obviously consensual nature of this event and to go to its own room at once, and then he accepted the kiss and returned it in full measure.

WAS IT POSSIBLE THAT HER dream of being a desired, beloved wife and mother might actually come true? Not with this man, unfortunately, who was just her therapist, but was she alluring after all, capable of attracting a man who would make the dream a reality?

Two long years of nothing, which included, of

course, the year with Sven, which was worse than nothing, because she had *someone* who was doing *nothing.* And here, at last, was a lifeline. Max must be an incredibly well-educated psychiatrist because he could kiss like no man she'd ever kissed, which admittedly hadn't been many, but she suspected she could kiss a thousand men and not enjoy it any more than she was enjoying this kiss, starting with the first electrical shock of contact. His mouth feathered over hers, then the two of them drew together with the inevitability of magnets. She shivered when his tongue flicked into the corners of her mouth and then tentatively moved inside her. The sensation whipped through her body, knocking out her ability to think or reason.

She writhed against him, dizzied by waves of pure animal wanting. She slid her hands around his neck to steady herself, then across his shoulders, down his back. Feeling his muscles clench beneath her touch only made her dizzier. His hands went to her waist, tugged her T-shirt upward and, with it, the camisole she wore beneath. It seemed absolutely essential to get him out of his clothes, too, but when she felt his lips against her bare breast, she lost interest in everything except what he was doing to her, outside and in.

His lips demanded and promised, took and gave. Her head fell back, and with a moan she resigned herself to savoring the feel of them, the sensations in her breasts as he caressed them, circling her nipples with his tongue, then tugging them into his mouth. There suddenly seemed to be plenty of time. She wasn't even close to losing her nerve. Just her mind.

Her breasts ached when he slid down between them, slid farther down. Last time she'd noticed, she'd been wearing a skirt. What had happened to it? But a second later she was delighted it had vanished. His fingertips stroked the silk of her panties, and a few strokes later, they seemed to have disappeared, too, and his mouth moved against her stomach, down through the mound of curls, generating the white-hot heat that flamed inside her. She arched her back to make the wonderful thing he was doing to her easier for him, so easy he would never stop, not even when, eventually, she begged him to.

But that moment never came, while Blythe did, over and over, crazed by the touch of his tongue, his lips, his smooth, firm fingertips, until at last she had ripped his black briefs off his body and convinced him to thrust himself inside her.

The resulting frenzy of mutual plundering left them crossways on the bed, her straddling him, his head and feet hanging off. As he pounded into her, she flipped them over so that he was on top. He thrust into her again and propelled them into the footboard, which obligingly fell off. They crashed to the floor on top of it.

From beneath them came the unmistakable sound of a broom handle knocking against the ceiling of the apartment below, the universal sign to quiet down. It distracted her just enough to allow a fleeting concern that Max was still conscious, but all her senses told her the only part of him she cared about at the moment still plunged into her and withdrew, plunged and withdrew. If it was merely a neurological impulse at work, she didn't care; it felt just as good. If he stopped, then she'd worry about restoring him to consciousness.

But he didn't stop, didn't even pause. A driving force built up more intensely inside her with each thrust. She was going to explode. With a shriek, she did, spasms shaking her from head to toe, tentative at first, then escalating so ferociously that she collapsed against him, wet with sweat, having barely enough energy left to observe that he still had plenty.

"The footboard wasn't holding up anything structural, was it?" His voice was rough, although his mouth wasn't as it nibbled at her neck. "We'll resume play on the field."

She emitted a small moan of protest as he rolled himself off the flattened footboard, picked her up in his arms and deposited her onto the tangled sheets. His skin was hot. "You're burning up," she said, stroking his chest. "You need to cool off."

"Someday." His arms tightened around her.

"I have an idea," she whispered, sliding out of bed, feeling him try to tug her back.

"A kinky one?"

"I have a personal fan," Blythe said, starting to search the darkness of her closet.

"Me."

She turned to direct a smile at him, even though she knew he couldn't see it. "Thank you," she said. "You're going to be a bigger fan in a minute."

"I'm already a bigger fan. Come back to bed."

But she'd found the battery-operated fan and turned it on herself as she took it back to the night table. "There. How's that?"

"Ahh, ohh," he moaned, and he must have stretched out his arms and legs directly out to his sides, because when she tried to climb in beside him, the only room in the bed was on top of him. "A dream come true."

"Uh-*huh*," she said as she settled herself over him, melting like frosting on a hot cake.

3

AT SOME POINT IN THE LONG, lovely night, Blythe made tuna fish sandwiches, which they fed to each other in bed. During another brief respite, Max limped to the kitchen in search of the cookie tin. When the fan ran out of battery power, they opened all the windows and took a cold shower together, Blythe's puckered nipples warming to the heat of Max's chest and his arousal undiminished by the icy spray.

There were forays for water, forays for fortifying fruit juices, but mainly there were forays into each other until, at last, too exhausted and sated to care about the stray bits of tuna fish and chocolate chunks, Blythe fell asleep in midkiss.

When she woke up, Max was propped up on one elbow, gazing down at her in a brightly lit room.

"Electricity?" she murmured sleepily, trying to burrow back into the hollow of his shoulder.

"Sun," he said, his voice low and warm. "It's after ten o'clock." His fingertip trailed lazily over her bare stomach, and Blythe instinctively tried to make her navel touch her tailbone. "How do you feel?"

"Fantastic. How do you feel?"

He hesitated a moment, still tracing her skin. "Fantastic...and surprised."

Blythe frowned into his shoulder. "What kind of surprise? Good surprise? Bad surprise?" He'd mentioned that in Candy's phone call, Blythe had sounded like a person with a lot of nerve, and admittedly, she'd put all the nerve she had into last night, but what if he'd expected more assertiveness? More imaginative ideas? More leather? Some, anyway?

There was a raspy chuckle in his voice. "Good surprise. Definitely. I mean, I'd hoped this would happen. You have to admit I came prepared."

"For an orgy," she muttered, thinking of the endless supply of condoms he'd reached for during the night, "but of course, a person in your position would have taken extra precautions. Besides, they were probably tax-deductible. Or maybe you get them free from salesmen."

He gave her an odd look. "Why would I get them free?"

"Because tonight, or last night, was business-related."

He found a bit of chocolate on her ear and licked it off, making her shiver. "I suppose you could call it business-related."

She grew very still. "Did it feel like more than business to you?" The words came timidly. "Because it did to me."

He buried his face in her neck. "It had nothing to do with business. In fact, if we're going to be working together, we have to keep this totally separate from business or I won't get any work done."

For the first time, Blythe felt that something might be a little bit wrong. She came fully awake.

"Yeah." He was talking to himself now and sounding nostalgic. "When you called—"

But she hadn't called him. Candy had.

"—and offered to welcome me personally to New York—"

Blythe stiffened. *Ooh.* A whole lot wrong.

"—I asked Bart about you and he said—"

How did he know Bart?

"'Candy Jacobsen? It should be quite a welcome.' So Bart's already expecting hanky-panky in the office and it would be a shame to disappoint—"

Blythe spun into a sitting position before she interrupted him. She needed to feel more on top of things. "*Candy?* You came *here* to do *this* with *Candy?*"

He sat up even straighter than she had and stared at her. "No, I came here to take you out on a date. Things happened. Like a blown transformer. And why are you referring to yourself in the third person?" With one foot he began to fish for something on the floor. In a second or two he brought those little black briefs up with his toes and slid them under the covers. The violent thrashing of the sheets and blankets was a dead giveaway that he was putting them on.

Blythe fished with her toes, too, and brought up the peach silk boxers and camisole he'd tossed to the floor the night before, which was beginning to feel like a lifetime ago. She struggled into them, babbling. "Because I'm very much afraid there is a third person! You were coming at seven o'clock. To help me get over Sven." She leaped out of bed, darted to her closet and pulled out a pair of flowered capris, tugging them clumsily up over the boxers, which felt as if she'd put them on backward.

When she turned back to face him, he was out of bed with one leg in his jeans and his arms folded across his chest. The black briefs had a ripped seam down the left side. She had a feeling they hadn't been ripped until *she* had ripped them off him. "Candy," he said slowly and grimly, "who's Sven?"

"I'm not Candy," she said desperately.

"Then who the hell are you?" He almost yelled the words.

"I'm Candy's roommate. You're supposed to be Candy's old friend, the sensitive psychiatrist from Boston who was coming here to shrink my sexual insecurities."

"I've never met Candy, and I am for sure not a psychiatrist." His eyes widened. "You were planning to do this with some other guy?"

"No, I wasn't, but then I met you and decided I would, and after last night, the other guy isn't necessary anymore. After last night—" she lowered her voice to a whisper "—I don't think I have sexual insecurities." She cleared her throat. "Ah, what line of work *are* you in, because I'm sure a psychiatrist couldn't have dealt with my problem any more sensitively than you did."

Glaring at her, he stepped out of the pants leg he'd just gotten into instead of putting on the jeans completely. Blythe was sure he had no idea he wasn't wearing anything but his ripped briefs while he gave her his full credentials, or that while his voice sounded cold, his erection persisted. "I'm Max Laughton, political columnist, formerly with the *Chicago Observer*, and starting Monday, with the *New York Telegraph*. And I should have guessed the *Telegraph* was a congenial place to work when Candy called and invited me out. I just couldn't believe it would be—" his voice deepened to a growl "—*quite this congenial!*"

The growl had almost built to a roar when a sound came from the living room, a sound that chilled Blythe to her very bones. The whoosh of the door opening and closing, followed by Candy's voice, which although it was a little out of breath, somehow projected across miles. "Come on in, Garth. I'll make the introductions and then I'll get cleaned up and skedaddle back down the frigging stairs so you two can go for it. Blythe?" It was a shout. "We're here. You okay?"

No! Not anymore! She'd stolen Candy's date, and there would be hell to pay.

She swallowed. "I'm fine," Blythe called. "I've been so worried about you!" With Candy safe and sound, she was considerably more worried about herself.

"I spent the night in the frigging office," Candy yelled. "Garth got caught on the wrong side of the Triborough Bridge and the frigging state patrol put him in a homeless shelter in Queens." Her voice seemed more distant. "He asked for a hotel and they said, 'Whadda ya think we are, a frigging travel agency?'" Blythe heard her laugh. "Hey! Good news! We bought coffee from a guy on the street cooking on frigging propane."

"Candy, really, your language." That must be whatshisname, Garth, speaking. He had a pleasant-sounding voice, but it didn't stroke her the way Max's voice did when he wasn't yelling at her.

"Is she coming in here?" Max crossed his hands over the crotch of his ripped briefs.

"I'm sure she wouldn't." Blythe suddenly snapped out of her stupor. "I'll be out in a minute," she shouted, making wild gestures at Max to "keep quiet" and "get dressed" and "keep quiet" again for good measure. "I, ah, overslept," she improvised. "Just throwing on some clothes."

While Max scrambled through the small bag he'd gotten the condoms out of—oh, Lord, the condoms they'd used—emerging with a pair of wildly patterned boxer shorts and a different pair of pants, tan slacks this time, she tugged a peach tank top over her head, then snagged her fingers in her tangled hair.

"Don't dress up for us." Garth again. "We look like we've spent the night in jail."

"Did you hear anything from my date?" Candy yelled. "I couldn't reach him. Did he show up here?"

"I'm very much afraid he did," Blythe said in her normal voice, sending a condemnatory glance in Max's direction, which was lost on him because he was concentrating on the buttons of a tan-and-blue striped shirt. One flew off. He snarled and reached into his bag, coming out with another shirt, this one navy.

"What did you say?" Candy yelled.

"I said we'll talk in a minute."

Blythe took a peek at herself in the mirror and groaned. She looked like, and undoubtedly reeked with, the scent of sex. She should have worn a bra under the tank top. Her nipples were sticking out through the camisole, but there wasn't time to do anything about her appearance. Directing another set of pushing and lip-slashing "stay back and keep quiet" gestures at Max, who was still ignoring her, she inched open the door and went out to face the music. Or rather, Candy and the psychiatrist, a pair she'd spent the night wronging.

"Hi," she said, smiling brightly.

"Oh, there you are," Candy called from the kitchen. "Garth, say hi to Blythe. Then would you light the frigging stove so we can keep the coffee warm? I'm doing something wrong. Blythe, what were you saying about my date?"

Blythe felt the blood draining from her face and realized Garth was staring at her, so she darted a glance at him. He was attractive, just as Candy had said, but his face didn't have the character, the punch Max's did. She scanned the rest of him while she tried to think of an answer to give Candy. His blondness was accentuated by a pale beige summer suit, badly creased, a light blue-striped shirt and a blue tie patterned in yellow— she squinted at it—ducks.

He didn't seem to notice how distracted she was. A sensitive man would have taken one look at her and called 9-1-1. Instead, he said over his shoulder as he went to save Candy from blowing up the building, "Wow. Candy told me you were a great-looking girl, but that was an understatement."

"Did he?" Candy said, stepping out of the kitchen as soon as Garth stepped in. "My date, Blythe. Did he show up?" She sounded impatient.

Candy also looked the worse for wear. The toes of her pointed shoes curled up and wrinkles made her linen skirt even shorter. There were deep circles under her eyes. She must have had a hard time getting back to the office and an uncomfortable night sleeping there, just to assure Blythe's privacy with Garth. Blythe's guilt grew and compounded.

Feeling the blood rush back to her face, Blythe said, "I...well, he..."

"All lit up," Garth said, returning to the living room.

"It just wasn't fair for that transformer to blow up yesterday," Candy said, pouting. "I had a date with Max Laughton, a dreamboat who's coming to the *Telegraph* from the *Chicago Observer*. Soon as I found out he'd been hired, I decided to get dibbies on him, because if he's half as hunky as his picture—"

A loud crash from Blythe's room caused both Candy

and Garth to swivel their heads toward the closed door. "Who's in there?" Candy asked in a hushed tone.

"Well," Blythe said, "I think it might be somebody trying to fix the bed. See, the strangest thing happened..."

"You broke your bed?"

"My, oh my, oh my," Garth murmured, gazing ceilingward.

"While I was trying to get Garth here to mend your psyche, you found somebody to break your frigging bed?" Candy's expression wavered between shock and admiration.

"Not exactly," Blythe mumbled.

"Then who—" Candy's eyes widened. "Oh, no. It couldn't be."

She whizzed past Blythe toward the closed bedroom door. Just as she reached it, it opened and Max strode out, wearing a navy blazer over his shirt and slacks. The crisp-cut outfit was a little incongruous with his unshaved face. Through the doorway, Blythe could see that he'd made up the bed and somehow put the footboard back on—upside down.

"Good morning," he said in a jarringly hearty tone. "Wow." He looked at Blythe, who stood quivering beside the sofa. "Either you slept on the *sofa* in your *clothes* or you sure were quiet when you came in to get them. I didn't wake up until I heard all the yelling."

He was a terrible liar, embarrassingly bad at it, but Blythe felt that was a point in his favor. He held out his hand to Garth. "I'm Max Laughton."

"Garth?" Garth said in a tentative sort of voice. "Garth Brandon? Dr. Garth Brandon." The title seemed to make him feel more secure.

Max shook Garth's hand briefly, then turned to

Candy. "You must be Candy. We had a date last night, and you're late." He gave her a totally engaging, disarming smile. Blythe would have died to be on the receiving end of that smile.

And was dying anyway, she was so touched to realize he was lying so unconvincingly in an attempt to save her reputation. A not-too-bright ape—and that would be according to ape standards—could have seen through him.

"Too late, apparently." Candy's chin firmed and her baby blue eyes flashed. "You slept together. I can see it written all over your faces. How could you, Blythe? You're my best friend."

In fact, a person could die from the sheer weight of the guilt Blythe felt on her shoulders.

"Let's have coffee!" Garth said. He smiled at all of them. He had a nice smile, but it didn't sock Blythe in the tummy the way Max's did. "We can sit down, have a cup and talk things over."

"There always were times, Garth," Candy snapped, "when your perfect manners made me want to frigging barf."

"Well, I'm sorry, Candy," Garth said. "I feel *used* by the thing that has obviously occurred, but it makes me feel more in control to act like a civilized human. Besides, as a psychiatrist I'm always open to understanding the deeper motivations of people in times of stress, so I think..."

"I'm warning you, Garth. Stop being so frigging nice or I'm going to upchuck," Candy said.

"Thank you for sharing your feelings," Garth said, escaping to the kitchen. "Cream, sugar, anyone?"

"I'll help," Blythe said. "Oh, look, you lit the oven, too. There's a coffee cake in the freezer. If I wrap it in foil, it will thaw in no time. And we have orange juice. Lots of sugar to jump-start the..."

"Listen to them," Candy said. "They're made for each other. And you had to come along and mess it up."

Max, who didn't want Blythe—that was her name, and it suited her—alone in the kitchen with this Garth person, was on his way to chaperone, but Candy's voice brought him to a halt with one foot in midair.

He settled it down to the floor, slowly turned back to her, and for the first time took a good long look at Candy Jacobsen, with whom he'd thought he was spending the night.

She had to be six feet tall in those witch's shoes she was wearing, and her blond hair, long and straight except where it curved at the ends, was thick and shiny.

Maybe a little too shiny. She wouldn't have been able to shower and wash it this morning at the *Telegraph* offices. The gunk on her eyes was half-on, half-off. Well, not off. It was still on her face, just not in the right places. Those dark circles under her eyes weren't exhaustion, they were eye makeup.

Who was he kidding? Cleaned up she'd be a stunner, a dream of a woman, just the kind of woman he was accustomed to dating, but more so. Then why did he keep glancing toward that kitchen door, hoping for another peek at the little red-haired, green-eyed Orphan Annie-type he'd—he'd—

It usually took him a few weeks to turn romance into a tangle that had to be straightened out. This time he'd done it before the first date.

"We can grill some toast," Blythe was saying. "It'll be good with the eggs."

"This is turning into a full breakfast," Garth answered her. "Maybe we should sit at the table."

"That's a good idea. I'll set the table while you finish up in here."

"No, no, I'll do it. You pour the juice."

Their happy voices were driving him crazy. "What exactly did I mess up?" he asked Candy, folding his arms across his chest and glaring at her.

"A perfect relationship," Candy snapped. "Blythe needed somebody to have sex with, sure, but I knew she and Garth would have more in common than sex. And—" she moved a step closer, smiling sexily at his angry expression "—I knew you and I would make sparks together." The smile faded. "And still will," she said with a determination that made Max nervous. He was trying desperately to put the set of unrelated facts together, read some sense into what was going on here.

"Sorry, it just didn't turn out that way," he said, trying to *look* sorry. "It was the blackout that messed it up, not me. I was here by invitation, *your* invitation," he reminded her, "but due to the circumstances, Blythe was the Good Samaritan who got me out of the elevator with her comb."

It must have been his mention of the comb that made her blink, because her anger only escalated. "A frigging *nameless* Good Samaritan, apparently?"

"I have to hand it to you, Candy," Garth said as he passed by, his hands filled with silverware. "You have toned down your language some."

"I can be ladylike when I want to," Candy snapped at him.

"I see," Garth said. He opened the drawer of a china cupboard and pulled out place mats. "Don't mind me." He tossed the words over his shoulder. "Keep talking. Communication is the key to successful relationships." He whipped a napkin into the shape of one of those flowers—calla lilies—and stood it up on the table. Max watched him, fascinated.

"You couldn't even take time for introductions?" Candy went on, her voice rising with her temper. "You just dragged her into the bedroom? And if you thought she was me, what led you to think you could drag me off to bed without the slightest..."

Blythe appeared with four glasses of juice on a tray. The juice sloshed as she jolted to a halt, her face going red again. Who dragged whom into the bedroom was not something Max intended to share with Candy. He wished he could reassure Blythe that he intended to take all the blame.

"No," Blythe spoke up, "that's not the way it happened at all. When he jumped off the elevator he said he had a blind date with somebody on the twenty-third floor. I had a blind date and I live on the twenty-third floor. So I thought he—" she jutted a thumb at Max from under the tray "—was you." She jutted her other thumb at Garth, who was still setting the perfect table.

"She was expecting a man and there he was," Garth said. "The man had been invited for a specific purpose, so when they got up here, she understandably assumed—"

"Garth, will you ever frigging learn to *express* your anger?" Candy said. "Stop sounding like marshmallow cream. I thought psychiatrists had to get psychoanalyzed themselves. Didn't you learn anything?"

"Blythe, hand me that juice," Max said. "While there's still some in the glasses."

"What Garth said," Blythe interrupted him, "was *how* it happened, but not *why* it happened." She passed the tray of juice to Max. He could tell she was intent on self-immolation.

"My, doesn't that coffee smell good," he said quickly, before she could pour on any more gasoline. "Garth is right. A jolt of caffeine will make everything look different."

"The juice glass goes directly above the point of the knife," Garth said kindly, redoing Max's arrangement of juice-glass-dead-center above the place mats, "and breakfast is ready! Yum!"

Was this guy for real?

"BLYTHE, YOU WERE about to say..." Candy helped herself to a square of coffee cake.

"Oh, yes." Blythe put down the fork she'd just picked up. She desperately wanted to get it all out in the open—not the intimate details, of course, just a full accounting of her despicable behavior and innocent motivations. "I was saying you still didn't understand exactly why it happened. It happened because I felt so guilty."

"You mean now. You feel so guilty now," Candy said, reaching for the butter.

"No," Blythe said. "I mean, yes, I feel guilty about you now, but then I was feeling guilty about Garth. I thought your idea was terrible, as you know, and I had no intention of going along with it—"

"You didn't?" Garth said. One small flicker of an eyebrow indicated the possibility of annoyance.

"What idea?" Max said.

"It will all become clear to you later," Candy said. "Let her finish her frigging sentence."

"I didn't see how you could have managed to reach him to cancel the date," Blythe said to Candy, "with the cell phone circuits all tied up and you maybe stuck on the subway in the dark where you couldn't get a circuit anyway. So I felt as if I'd rejected him before I ever met him or got to know him." With her clasped hands, Blythe implored Candy to understand. "I didn't even know his name! And I was imagining him in a plane with no place to land and running out of gas and about to crash, and I felt so bad that I hadn't even given him a chance, and here he'd died trying to reach me and save my psyche—the psyche of a total stranger who wasn't even paying him by the hour—that when he wasn't dead, as I could clearly see when he jumped out of the elevator on top of me, I wanted to make it up to him." She sent anxious glances toward each of them. She couldn't imagine what she'd said to make them look so stunned.

"Aw," Garth said. "That's sweet."

"Could you run that past me again?" Candy's eyes narrowed. "The part about Max jumping you?"

Blythe was grateful when Max spoke up. "It was dark and I was scared sh—to death. I just wanted out of that elevator. I didn't think about where I was jumping. Or who. As I recall, I threw my duffel bag out first. It might have knocked Blythe senseless even before I jumped out with my briefcase. It was a totally accidental jumping, motivated by fear, not craven lust. You can probably understand that, Garth."

"I don't," Candy spoke up.

"Garth will explain it to you," Max said.

"Explain what?" Garth said.

Candy's gaze zeroed in on Blythe. "It didn't occur to you to tell him your name, like, 'Hi, I'm Blythe,' and then Max would have said, 'Oh, sorry, my date is with Candy on the twenty-third floor'?"

"No," Blythe said in a small voice. "I just assumed I was the person he came here to—"

"Meet," Max said firmly.

Candy snorted inelegantly and served herself scrambled eggs.

"You can imagine how guilty I felt by then. I mean he wasn't dead, but he was nearly dead, so I thought it was up to me to offer him hospitality."

"She was very hospitable," Max contributed. At once, his skin darkened. Blythe thought it was probably as close as he could come to blushing.

"What's done is done," Garth pontificated. "We can't change the past."

Blythe was thinking hard. She owed Candy so much, and instead she'd betrayed her. No wonder Candy was furious. Garth was right. They couldn't change the past. Only the future. And Max must have realized how gorgeous Candy was. How could he help falling for her? How conflicted he must feel, knowing he could have spent the night with Candy. The ache of desire that had stayed with her through the nightmarish morning faded, replaced by an ache of pure sadness.

Blythe didn't want to do what she had to do, but she did have to do it. "Garth said it just right," she started, struggling to sound as if she meant it. "A mistake happened, and it happened at a time of crisis, when people don't always behave like their usual selves. I'm terribly sorry, Candy. I hope you'll forgive me, because... because..." Here came the hard part, and she didn't know how she was going to get through it. A set of images ran through her head—images of the glorious night with Max versus images of losing a friend of many years, an apartment she couldn't otherwise afford. Hard as she tried, the images of the night with

Max kept pushing aside her friendship with Candy and the comforts of her current lifestyle, but she couldn't let them win. They'd fade eventually, and everyday life would seem more important. Yes, it would. Definitely. Wouldn't it?

She pulled herself together. "Because," she said, "I'm not going to see Max again. He's all yours."

4

SILENCE AT THE BREAKFAST table followed Blythe's pronouncement, except for a low sound that came from Max's direction. She couldn't look at him.

"What maturity in such a young person," Garth said. "I hope your plans include starting over with me, too. Like tonight." He glanced at Candy, then sent a warm smile toward her.

Starting over with Garth wasn't part of the deal. Not after last night with Max. "I don't need to start over with anybody," Blythe blurted out. "I'm cured." She clapped a hand over her mouth, but it was too late.

"Of what?" Max's head swiveled toward her.

"Of—" Candy said.

"Of my need to have a blind date with anybody, ever again." Blythe leaped up from her chair so vigorously that it fell over with a crash. She ran a hand through her hair, feeling what a tangled mess it was, and paced back and forth behind the fallen chair. "My goodness, look at the trouble it has caused! From now on, I'm not going out with anybody until I've known him for years. Okay, Garth? I'll check back in with you after I've known you for years. So let's say no more about it!" She tugged Max's still-filled plate out from under his raised fork. He snatched it back.

"Don't be silly, Blythe," Candy said. "You and Garth

can have a nice platonic evening together if that's what you want."

"Of course," Garth said. "I'm going to be here through the weekend. I'd just like a little company, especially since Candy's going to be busy."

There was another low sound from Max. Blythe worried that he was Mount Vesuvius, about to blow.

"Where'd you get these eggs?" Garth said. "They taste like the ones my mother used to get at the Farmers' Market. And this coffee cake—it has to be homemade. I was right there in the kitchen. I saw the wrappings. Unless you're into rewrapping to impress your guests." He gave her a teasing smile.

"Never," she said, not smiling back. "I never rewrap."

"For God's sake, Garth, this is a big moment," Candy said. "Get off the just-like-Mom-used-to-make kick." She sounded cross.

"Actually, I've got to get going," Garth said. "I've got to give a paper this afternoon, power or no power."

"On what?" Max said in a flat voice.

"I'm presenting a paper on the psychological effects of alternative-lifestyle teachers on first-grade students."

"Really." Max was staring at Garth. "And what are the psychological effects?"

"None," Garth said.

"So it's all settled," Candy said. "I'll go out with Max and Blythe will go out with Garth."

"All settled," Garth said.

"All settled," Blythe echoed, hearing her voice echo dully.

"Not *quite.*"

Now Blythe had to look at Max. His expression was

calm enough, but his eyes were stormy. She sent him a pleading look, imploring him to make this easier for her. Who knew what might happen in time, but for now, she just wanted to get rid of her guilt and make peace.

If he cared at all how she felt, he'd go along. And if he didn't, well, then he wasn't worth waiting for.

MAX WAS SO MAD HE ALMOST wished he'd stayed on the elevator. He'd put all the pieces of the puzzle together now, and he understood what was going on. Apparently Candy had brought Garth here to deal with some sexual insecurities Blythe supposedly had after a relationship with a scumbag named Sven, but Blythe had told him in her own words that he, Max, had done a perfectly good job dealing with those insecurities and she didn't have them anymore. So she didn't, absolutely did not, need Garth. And it was out of the question that he should go out with Candy.

Okay, maybe Blythe wasn't drop-dead gorgeous like Candy. He'd call her…adorable. Yes. That was it. Small and soft and creamy and luscious like a perfectly ripened peach, the kind that had come in those Fruit-of-the-Month boxes his boss at the *Chicago Observer* had given his minions for Christmas one year.

She'd been all his for a single night, and he was already wondering if the reactions going on in his body might move gradually toward his mind. Like, could she be the woman he'd like to spend a lifetime with?

Not if she refused to go out with him again. That was really making him mad. He wasn't up for auction. He was an adult capable of making his own decisions, and he'd decided he wanted to put some effort into a relationship with Blythe.

And nobody, nobody was telling him he couldn't.

Except Blythe, of course, and that's what she had just told him. He felt like snarling.

The question was why. She'd had just as good a time last night as he had. It was her roommate who was spooking her. Sure it was bad manners to steal somebody else's guy or girl, but that wasn't really what had happened here. But it had made Candy mad, and Candy mad seemed to scare Blythe out of all proportion.

If Candy got really mad, one of them could find another apartment. Simple as that. So something more was at stake here. He could see it in Blythe's eyes, the way she was looking at him, begging him to go along with the promise she'd just made Candy.

Okay, he could cooperate until he figured out why Candy ruled this roost. Then he could show Blythe why she didn't have to let Candy rule. So what was he going to say instead of what he'd been about to say, which had been way too direct?

"This isn't a consensus thing," he said, trying to sound like a psychiatrist himself. "It's a freedom of choice thing."

He saw Blythe halt in her hyperactive table-clearing, standing stock-still with a butter dish poised in one hand and the egg platter in the other.

"You're right, of course," Candy said. "And I choose to turn in my rain check and go out with you tonight."

"My turn," Garth said. "I choose to take Blythe out this evening and get to know her better."

"I choose...I choose..." Blythe said, "I choose for everybody to be happy."

"Then we'll all go out together," Max said.

"A double date?" Candy sounded appalled. He

wasn't surprised. He'd dashed her hopes for a hot night with the new guy in town.

Garth, on the other hand, seemed intrigued by the idea. "That's brilliant, Langston," he said.

"Laughton," Max said.

"Laughton," Garth repeated. "We won't call it a double date, Candy. It will be four friends going out together."

"Ooh, I can hardly wait," Candy muttered.

Max looked at Blythe for approval, but her expression was inscrutable.

"Oh, okay," Candy said as if she'd been arguing with someone. "We'll meet here at seven o'clock for a drink and then go on to dinner. Blythe will put some hors d'oeuvres together for us, won't you, Blythe, and dinner if we can't find a restaurant open?"

"Well, I..."

"They won't need you at the *Telegraph* today," Candy went on. "I'm going to pop back over there as soon as I clean up."

"So I'll just..." Blythe said.

Max gave her a glare, intending to suggest that she speak up, stop being such a wimp, but she was ignoring him and the only part of the situation he understood was that she didn't want him talking back to Candy.

"So if you'd let Garth use your shower," Candy said to Blythe, "the three of us could leave together."

"I'm going to try to get a cab," Max said. "Garth, I'll drop you at your hotel on the way to my new apartment." *Or out the window on your head.*

"Garth's staying here," Candy said.

Max gazed at her, then at Garth, then at Blythe, who gave him a tenuous smile. "I'm leaving," Max said.

"Oh, come on," Candy said, "it won't take us a minute, will it, Garth?"

"I'm leaving now," Max said, and did.

THE SUNSHINE THAT illuminated the room seemed to dim after Max left. To get her mind off him, Blythe began clearing the table in earnest.

Candy flounced off to her own room and closed the door. Two hard thumps indicated that she'd kicked off her shoes. "Leave the dishes," Garth said. "I'm sorry Candy was so bossy about the shower. I think she takes charge because nobody else in her house ever took charge. Doesn't mean we have to do what she says. You shower first. I'll get started on the dishes."

Blythe gazed at him, thinking he was probably a really nice man who might be a really good friend. "That's okay," she said, and smiled at him. "I'm not going to work today, and I know you're anxious to get to your conference, start meeting people, all those conference things. But thanks for asking."

She sneaked in and made Candy's bed while Candy was still splashing in the shower. When she heard water running from her own bathroom, she slipped silently into her bedroom. Max had made her bed in a rather unorthodox way, but she changed the sheets anyway, keeping a wary eye toward the bathroom where Garth was singing "I Did It My Way" while he showered. He was flat. Garth was, she thought, rather flat, unlike Max, who was...

Not a good idea to think about Max. When he left, he'd been mad at all of them, especially at herself. He'd probably turn out to be a one-night stand after all. She fluffed up the sofa cushions by banging them violently against the coffee table and started on the dishes. She was scouring the sink when Garth and Candy appeared almost simultaneously, both of them clean, fresh and groomed to perfection. It must have been a requirement in their neighborhood. Blythe felt a refreshed awareness of her tangled hair and tossed-on clothes, and especially of her house slippers. They looked like a pair of tiger cubs and had been a Christmas gift from Candy.

"You finished the dishes," Garth said. "I was going to help you with them."

Candy gave him a sharp look. "We'll see you later," she said to Blythe. She didn't sound mad anymore, for which Blythe was grateful. "Just relax today and take it easy."

"Sure thing," Blythe said, already worrying about hors d'oeuvres.

MAX DID, IN FACT, get a cab. He got out on Broadway, intending to shop his way home—an old-fashioned phone that didn't require electricity and snacks to go with drinks tonight being his top priorities. Damned if Blythe was going to spend the day cooking. But everything was closed except one drugstore operating on a cash-only basis, and they were flat-out of phones, portable radios and batteries. They did have enormous cans of pretzels and mixed nuts, though. He bought one of each, added some other snacks and bottled water for himself and, burdened with his purchases as well as his luggage, he strolled on toward the apartment he'd bought during the quick trip he'd made to New York in February to interview for, then accept the job with the *Telegraph*.

He'd never felt so out of touch in his life. Being without newspapers—now that was weird. Newspapers had been a standard fixture in his life from the day he was born. They'd been his father's life, and he'd followed in his father's footsteps.

Well, not quite. He was going for the big time, while his dad was happy as an ant in honey in that little town on the western border of New Jersey as the editor and publisher of a small regional weekly newspaper. His mom covered the weddings and did a recipe column with a theme—"Pot Luck, Please," or "Cold Weather Comforts." But those were just hobbies for her. What she really liked was keeping the house running smoothly and putting great meals on the table, and she didn't apologize for it, either.

Didn't make 'em like Mom anymore. Now and then Max indulged himself in the faint hope he might find a woman whose career wasn't the most important thing in her life, but he'd pretty much given up on that idea. Now he'd be happy just to find a woman he didn't instantly start looking for a tactful way to break up with.

That was how he got into trouble with women. Wanting to break up with them and hating to hurt their feelings. He was already in that spot with Candy, and he hadn't even gone out with her yet. Wasn't going to, either, if he could help it.

He'd managed a call to his folks to tell them he'd gotten to LaGuardia before it shut down, and planned to hoard whatever power his cell phone had left until he could hook up the charger, but an intense urge to call Blythe overtook him. Hell, he needed to call her, tell her he had the hors d'oeuvres covered. And to yell at her some for making a really stupid decision that involved both of them. So he dialed the home number Candy had given him, but it just rang and rang. They probably didn't have old-fashioned phones, either.

He had absolutely nothing to do with his frustration but call the guy who was even now trying to bring him his worldly goods on a moving van. It turned into quite a lengthy call. Tiger Templeton of Smooth Moves knew more about the blackout and its aftermath than Max did. The bridges and tunnels into New York were opening one at a time, but the traffic was so heavy, cars being the only means of transportation into the city right now, that he wouldn't consider delivering Max's shipment today. Not even if he were anywhere close to Manhattan, which he wasn't. Tiger's van had thrown a rod, and he still had to drop off a third of a truckload to a little old lady in Cincinnati. His best guess was tomorrow, Saturday. That is, unless his second drop-off, to an antiques dealer in upstate New York, gave him any problems, in which case it would be Sunday.

Max set a new goal, to be the kind of man whose stuff would fill a whole moving van. It meant learning to spend money on furniture—big, van-filling furniture—which didn't sound like a whole lot of fun. This was one of those areas in which a wife would come in handy. Women liked to decorate, even when they also liked to work. He just liked to work.

He dropped his luggage and purchases off at his empty, lonely-looking new digs, cleaned himself up and walked the forty blocks south to the *Telegraph* building to settle uneasily into his new job.

WITH CANDY AND GARTH OUT the door at last, Blythe retreated to the shower. She turned her face up to let the water belt it with full force, and the hard-hitting spray reminded her at once of Candy. She and Candy had worked out a relationship, and until now, she'd thought it was mutually satisfactory. Candy had invited Blythe to share the apartment, a very nice apartment by New York standards, for a mere quarter of the rent. Since Blythe relished housework, cooking, shopping, decorating—all the domestic skills—and Candy didn't, what could be more natural than for Blythe to perform those tasks in return for the many, many things Candy had done for her? Of course, even people with domestic staffs often made their own beds and shoveled out their own bathrooms after dressing in the morning.

The flash of bitterness startled Blythe so much she inhaled sharply and nearly drowned. Choking and snortling, she asked herself why she was suddenly feeling resentful about a lifestyle she'd learned to take for granted.

It had something to do with the night she'd spent with Max, a night in which he'd given her everything he had to give without asking anything in return. He'd even made the bed, or tried to. She sensed that Max would never treat her like a servant just because she couldn't advance above proofreader-rewriter level at the *Telegraph.* Just because she couldn't afford half the rent of a four-thousand-dollar-a-month apartment.

She turned off the shower with an uncharacteristically vicious turn of the handle. She wouldn't default on her current contract, her contract with Candy that now included not seeing Max, but she would certainly seek out a new one.

Living in a hovel between Ninth and Tenth Avenues in Hell's Kitchen—and seeing Max—suddenly didn't sound half-bad. In fact, she could probably make a hovel look pretty cute. With Max in it.

The electricity went on at two o'clock in the afternoon. It meant she didn't have to beat the miniature quiche filling by hand. It might mean she was needed at the *Telegraph* again. Well, let them beg her to come back. But the afternoon passed, and nobody did.

CANDY SAT CLOSE TO MAX on the sofa and offered him a tiny quiche. "Yummy," she purred.

"Thank you," Blythe said rather sharply. It was killing her to see Candy snuggled up beside Max on the sofa. Apparently, according to Candy, the two of them had hung out together at the newsroom most of the day. When he'd stepped into the apartment looking wary, Blythe had felt a stab of intense longing that increased her dread of the outcome of this evening.

"We'll just save those pretzels and nuts for another occasion," Candy said. "But you were so sweet to bring them."

"I don't know how you did all this without electricity until the last minute," Garth said, nursing Blythe's earlobe between his thumb and index finger. The man who'd been so nice that morning, who'd promised to be such a good friend, had somehow turned into a lecher at his conference.

Blythe shot up out of the chair whose arm Garth was occupying, almost losing her ear. "May I freshen your drinks?" she said.

Max shot up just as abruptly from the sofa. "I'll get the booze."

His tone had a certain shock effect on the ambience. Candy, who'd been leaning against Max, and Garth, who'd practically fallen into the armchair when Blythe vacated it, both sat up a little straighter.

"Ooh," Candy said, "I love a man who takes charge."

"I took charge of serving the hors d'oeuvres," Garth said, sounding competitive.

"That's right. You did." Candy gave him an approving look. "And I'm sure Blythe appreciated it very much, didn't you, Blythe?"

"When's our reservation?" Moving faster than the speed of light, Max thrust a glass of Perrier at Garth.

"Seven-thirty," Blythe said. "I ordered a car service to pick us up at seven-fifteen. I wasn't sure what the taxi situation would be like."

"Seven-fifteen. Gee whiz, it's almost—" Max flipped his left wrist over to look at his watch "—six-fifteen. One more round of drinks and we'd better..."

Candy's little shriek drowned out his words. He'd been taking her a glass of chardonnay in the same hand he'd just flipped over. Now he looked down at the wet spot spreading across the short blue skirt she wore with a sheer, ruffly top, a bemused expression on his face as if he couldn't imagine how she'd gotten so wet.

"You're not a man who can hold his liquor," Blythe said with a giggle she recognized as verging on hysteria.

Max gave her an inscrutable glance. "Sorry," he said to Candy. "I'll get you another glass."

In a swift mood change, Candy stood up, moved so close to him she was almost molding her all-too-obvious nipples against his chest, wiggled her eyebrows and batted her lashes. "Not until you get me into dry clothes," she said.

Blythe sank back into the armchair and patted her forehead with a damp cocktail napkin.

"Blythe," Garth said solicitously, "are you all right?"

"I feel a little faint," Blythe said.

"Oh, come on," Candy said, moving a millimeter away from Max. "You can't be pregnant yet."

Blythe heard the hiss of air pass through Max's perfect teeth before he snaked away into the kitchen.

"Actually, she could," Garth said. "You see, Candy..."

"Will you shut up?" On her way to her room, presumably to put on another adorable little skirt and see-through top, Candy whirled. "Honest to God, Garth, now I remember what you were like as a kid. The rest of us would be running loose in the neighborhood, getting into all kinds of trouble, but not you. You'd be tagging around behind us saying things like, 'Do you know there are a billion jillion molecules in just one of those apples you're about to steal from Mrs. Greenbaum?' I mean, who cares how many—" She stopped very suddenly. "I should have known," she said, becoming sweet and kind, "that you'd become something smart and scientific, and you have. And Blythe really appreciates intelligent men."

"Oh..." Sounding pleased, Garth made a self-deprecating gesture with his hand.

Candy's door closed behind her and simultaneously, Max materialized at Blythe's side. "Take a sip of this," he said, handing her a glass of ice and water. "You'll feel better. It's still sort of hot in here."

She looked up at him and was startled when he gave her a slight wink. Maybe he wasn't mad at her after all. Maybe he understood why she had to give him up. She took a sip, then a deep, choking breath. It wasn't water, it was straight vodka, the hundred-proof kind they kept in the freezer. "Thank you," she said. "This ought to do it all right." She took a strengthening gulp, feeling the warmth travel straight through her.

"So, Garth." Max captured the other armchair, leaned forward and gazed raptly at the man. "I can see you were destined to spend your life helping others become more self-aware. Tell us about your practice. Families mainly, or children?"

Blythe blinked hard and choked down some more vodka, but Garth apparently didn't see anything but sincerity in Max's question.

"Couples," Garth said, looking saintly. "Women with low self-esteem, men who..."

An hour of the minutest details of the troubles of eleven dysfunctional couples later, the building intercom buzzed. "That must be the car service," Candy said, yawning prettily. She'd changed into a short blue-flowered skirt and blue tank top that matched her eyes. "Let's get going."

"...better communication, which usually solves the..." Garth continued as they sped toward the elevator bank.

BLYTHE GAZED AT THE MENU. It took her a minute to gather it up out of the foggy blur into which her eyesight had degenerated, but when she sorted out the letters and numerals, she could see that every item on it cost a thousand dollars. Well, it didn't, but on her budget a fourteen-dollar salad might as well have been a thousand-dollar salad.

The restaurant was so white, so spare and so brightly lit that she could see its details pretty clearly. From proofreading the lifestyle sections of the *Telegraph*, Blythe knew this was the trendy minimalist design for restaurants and hotels. She couldn't personally understand why a space that could double as an interrogation room had become *the* place to eat and sleep, but supposed it had something to do with Protestant guilt. Or Catholic guilt. Or Jewish. Some kind of guilt, anyway.

She glanced across the table at Max, who was gazing at the menu with the first show of happiness she'd seen from him since the night before. "It says," he said, "we should each order a main dish and two side dishes and we share all the side dishes. Okay, tonight was my idea and it's my treat. Live it up, folks."

Blythe barely had time to stifle a sigh of relief before Garth spoke up. "I'd intended to be the host tonight." Again Blythe heard that little competitive edge in his voice.

"Another time," Max said. "After all, this, ah, mix-up was all my fault."

Candy turned her gaze on Blythe and said, "You had help."

"Not really," Max said. "I've been thinking it over. If I'd said, 'I have a date with Candy Jacobsen' instead of 'I have a date with a woman on the twenty-third floor,' it would never have happened."

"Why didn't you?" Candy's voice was suddenly cold.

"For security reasons," Max said firmly.

It shut her up, as the word *security* tended to do these days. And a good thing, too, *security* being the reason for all sorts of outrageous inconveniences. He was getting pretty sick of Candy's constant digs at Blythe, frankly, dangerously sick. He was thinking of doing something about it.

"And based on your phone call," Max said, using a firm, cool voice and giving her a firm, cool smile, "I wasn't surprised by the reception Blythe gave me."

"Are you casting aspersions on Candy's reputation?" Garth said tightly just as a waiter appeared at their table.

"Get thish man a white horsh," Blythe told the waiter. It was the first time she'd spoken since she'd downed the vodka he'd given her, and Max observed that she wasn't speaking very clearly.

"With gin or vodka, sir?"

"She was only joking," Garth said. "Making a little reference to my gallantry. Knight on a white horse, you know." He smiled a modest smile. "I'll have a glass of red wine." He returned to glaring at Max.

"I'm dying for a Sour Apple Martini," Candy said.

Max focused his attention on Blythe. Her eyelids were drooping and her mouth seemed even fuller and more luscious than it had earlier. He'd brought her the vodka thinking it would help her relax, but he hadn't intended to knock her out.

"Madame?" The waiter was looking impatiently at Blythe.

"I'll have..."

"She'll have Pellegrino with lime," Max said, noticing that Blythe had folded her cocktail napkin into a little rose and had stuck it between her breasts. She was wearing a sedate black pantsuit with a short jacket, sedate except for the fact that she wasn't wearing a blouse under it and was showing a lot of cleavage. He gave the napkin flower a slight nod of approval. Whatever it indicated about her general sanity and sobriety, or lack thereof, it did cover some of the swell of her breasts.

"And so will I," he said in a hurry, feeling himself getting hard just thinking about Blythe's firm, round, full breasts, delicious handfuls of creamy flesh.

"I do not want Perraglino," Blythe said. "I want a Sour Apple, too."

"She'll have water," Max said. He'd made his decision and he intended to stick to it. This was the first time he'd ever gotten a woman drunk. He felt terrible about it, and didn't intend to take his eyes off her until he'd gotten her sober again.

"Yes, sir." The waiter dismissed himself.

"How dare you," Blythe said. She pointed a finger at him, which first waggled crazily, then made a downward curve.

"It was easy," Max said.

"How could you be drunk?" Candy asked. "You didn't drink anything. You hardly ever do."

Blythe frowned. "That, I think, is the plobrem. I need to get back in training, not that I've ever been in training for heavy drinking so I guesh...guess I shouldn't have said 'back in training,' but I'm doing it now, building up my resish...stance, even as we speak."

"Let's take a look at the menu," Max said. "Yumbo. I'm going to have this pork thing with the couscous. Candy?" Robotlike, he turned to her.

"Spoken like a true carnivore," Candy purred. She leaned closer to him, gripped his knee and slid her hand up his thigh. "I'll have the chicken with the chipotle chile sauce. You thought I couldn't get any hotter, didn't you? But just you wait."

Now her hand was dangerously close to the throbbing erection that was the product of Blythe's cleavage, the adorably resentful gaze she was still giving him because he'd insisted she drink water and a flood of memories from the night before. He couldn't think of anything to do but grip Candy's hand tightly as a way of restraining her. For his own comfort and pleasure, he wiggled his foot across the floor until it touched Blythe's little foot in its bright red shoe.

She jumped. "Chopopo chiles aren't all that hot," she said. "You should know that, Candy." She closed her eyes and stuck an index finger onto the menu. "I'll take this."

Garth leaned much too close to her for Max's comfort. He was close enough to look down the neckline of her jacket all the way to her... "Scallops in white wine sauce," he said in the tone of a man who wouldn't dream of looking down a woman's jacket. "That sounds great."

"I hate scallops," Blythe said. "Well, I don't hate them, but they're so white and insipid, and I say, why eat them when there are so many foods with adi...attitude? Why are you forsh...making me have scallops."

"Nobody's forcing you," Garth said with a knowing little smile, and angled his body closer to hers.

Max froze. He was not a violent man. True, he'd once beaten a computer to gravel when the entire set of font commands fused and he couldn't type in anything but twelve-point Monotype Corsiva—a small, pale, fake script he'd have to wear glasses to proofread. Those in charge at the *Chicago Observer* had forgiven him. After all, he was their star political columnist, it was an election year and he was on a tight deadline. But now he was wondering if the *New York Telegraph* would overlook his committing a felony, because what he wanted to do was pound Garth into gravel. He'd swear on the diamond earrings his father had given his mother for their twenty-fifth anniversary that Garth's left hand was angled perfectly for exploring Blythe's right knee, and that could make any man want to kill.

Instead of killing, he slid the toe of his shoe over her instep, across her ankle and up her leg.

He wasn't playing footsie. He was trying to send her a this-too-shall-pass message. He was also hoping to run across Garth's hand and while he was at it, he'd break every knuckle in it.

"Blythe will have the venison tournedos with the pomegranate-molasses glaze," Max said as he steered his foot closer and closer to the knee on which he was sure Garth's hand rested. "I suggest we move on to a neutral topic."

"World peace?" Candy said, sounding very dry and also very sober in spite of the three glasses of wine she'd had at home and the Sour Apple Martini she'd just downed.

Max aimed a condemnatory glare at her flippancy. "We're having a dinner that would feed an entire country. Let's go for hunger in third-world nations."

"De-pressing," Candy moaned.

They might think she was tipsy, but Blythe hadn't missed a thing that was going on. Candy was hitting on Max, Garth was hitting on her and somebody's foot was climbing her leg.

"Pomegranate molasses?" she murmured. "What's—" But nobody was listening.

"...an admirable American trait to send shipments of food to the very country we're bombing..."

That's what the noble Garth was saying at the very moment he was digging five perfectly manicured fingernails into her right kneecap. But that had to be Max's foot climbing her leg. It couldn't be Garth's foot unless he was a psychiatrist-contortionist. And she certainly couldn't ask him if he was a psychiatrist-contortionist, because her tongue was too numb.

"...seems to me agricultural training is the answer..."

"...but not the only answer. Birth control..."

The problem with Garth's fingernails in her kneecap, which he undoubtedly thought was driving her into a frenzy of passion, was that her kneecaps were excruciatingly ticklish.

"...thousands dead," Max was saying somberly just as she couldn't hold it back any longer and began to giggle.

Once she'd started, she couldn't stop. Tears filled her eyes. "Awful, isn't it?" she snorted through the hideous sounds burbling up her throat. "All those poor people..."

The conversation came to a halt.

"Blythe," Garth said, sounding shocked.

"For God's sake, Blythe," Candy muttered. "Pull yourself together."

Max merely gave her a puzzled look. But of course he didn't know she was ticklish. He hadn't tickled her at all last night, although she was sure he'd touched her knees and slid his hands down her rib cage. Last night, she'd forgotten she was ticklish.

It swam back into her consciousness, the whole night, and the giggles faded away. She gazed at him across the table, at his strong, neat features, his dark hair, his dramatically blue eyes, remembering the feel of his mouth against hers.

Garth was a scallop. That was a certainty. And Max was venison tournedos with a pomegranate-molasses glaze. She'd never eaten venison tournedos glazed with pomegranate molasses, but she imagined them to be meaty yet tender, with just the right touch of sweetness. And her mouth watered for him. Them.

She didn't want scallops. If she didn't want to end up in an uncomfortable situation with Garth this evening, she had to be strong. She made a face at the Pellegrino, but she drank it.

The meal was delicious. Her wooziness had diminished, and she'd just begun to feel that everything might somehow come out all right in the end when Candy said, "Excuse me. Powder room. Blythe, want to join me?"

"Sure," Blythe said, extricating her foot from Max's and her knee from Garth's grip in order to get up. The message in Candy's tone had been clear. Candy wanted to talk to her.

Blythe's heart did a little pitter-pat. Maybe Candy had sensed the sizzle between Blythe and Max, and was giving up on the idea of having him for herself. So she trotted along behind Candy into the small, brightly lit rest room, which truly did feel like an interrogation room, instinctively glanced into the mirror and frowned. "What on earth is this?" she said, tugging a crumpled napkin out from between her breasts.

"It's not important. Here's what we're going to do. I'm going to take Max back to his place and you're going home with Garth. Got it?"

5

CANDY'S DIRE PRONOUNCEMENT pounded against Blythe's eardrums. The blood rushed so rapidly from her face to her toes that she thought she might faint. Why, why had she let Candy intimidate her into making that stupid promise not to see Max again?

But she had made the promise, and now had to go home with Garth while Candy worked her wiles on Max. The outcome was inevitable. Max would fall under Candy's spell and forget Blythe very quickly. What man could resist Candy's open, honest, lustful pursuit of pure pleasure, no strings attached?

Or maybe Candy was already thinking strings. And just to rub the maximum amount of salt into the wound, she'd probably ask Blythe to be her maid of honor. Then she'd triple the humiliation by choosing the most hideous bridesmaids' dresses on the market, and Blythe's would be...mauve.

She couldn't make it through the wedding. Sure as anything, when the minister asked for reasons why these two should not be joined together, she would yell, "Because he's mine! I had him first."

Blythe had left the table with a hopeful heart and a light step. Now she plodded back in Candy's wake. The men were fighting over the bill. Max was apparently winning. Graciously he allowed Garth to contribute the tip.

"Garth, run Blythe back to the apartment, will you?" Candy said when the negotiations ended. "I need to powwow with Max. I'm sure there are ways a political columnist can interface with a crime reporter." She winked at Blythe.

"Sure," Blythe murmured, feeling numb. "Come on, Garth. Let's go."

Max gave her a sharp glance. "We're all very tired, I'm sure," he said. "It would be better to go to our own homes and get a good night's rest. I'm sure Candy told you Bart has asked us all to work over the weekend, get caught up."

"I guess I forgot," Candy said. "But don't worry," she said to Max. "I'll get you there bright and early in the morning." She batted her eyelashes.

"Fine," Blythe said. Unable to bear the way Max was looking at her, she stood up. "Come on, Garth," she said.

As Blythe stepped into the back seat of a taxi, she saw Candy climbing into a taxi with Max. Which meant Max hadn't said no to her.

But then, so few people did.

Garth was watching Candy and Max, too. "Whew, that was tense," he said, removing the arm he'd slid insidiously along the ledge behind them.

Blythe stared at him. "It's a tense situation all around," she said.

"A dumb situation, if you ask me," Garth said. "Why is she so determined to go after this guy? She doesn't know him. This morning she said she asked him out after she saw his picture. Now, I ask you. What can you tell from a picture?" He slumped against the seat.

"She could tell he was very good-looking," Blythe

explained, wondering why she was having to explain anything to Garth. "We don't have a lot of good-looking available men to go out with so she wanted to grab him first. She's very competitive. You must know that."

"But you two clearly hit it off. Why didn't she give up on him? I mean, what's so special about Max that she'd insist on having her chance with him?"

Blythe sat up very straight. "What's so *special* about him? Everything! He's wonderful to look at, fun to talk to, a fabulous—" she caught herself just in time "—political columnist," she said instead of "lover."

"What do you mean, 'wonderful to look at'? He's just an ordinary guy."

What in the world was wrong with him? Was he that mad that he wasn't getting anywhere with her? After all those moves in the restaurant, now he wasn't acting like a man who had the slightest interest in going to bed with her. He wasn't acting like the man he'd been this morning, either, a patient and reasonable psychiatrist-type.

"He's a whole lot more than just an ordinary guy," she said hotly. "He's gracious and thoughtful and generous and—"

"You folks want to get out or just go on fighting," interrupted the cab driver.

Blythe and Garth each tried to shove a bill over the back of the seat, and did it so vehemently their wrists collided painfully. Garth's arm was longer. It was his bill the driver took, and Garth flung open the door.

"You don't know any of those things about him for sure," he argued, rubbing his wrist. "You only met him twenty-four hours ago. And you've seen more of him than Candy has. She doesn't know anything about him. I bet," he said, storming into the building, "he's the kind of guy who lays on the charm, leads women on and then just walks away, leaving them broken-hearted and thinking it was all their fault, something they did wrong."

"I may not have known him long, but I'm absolutely certain he's not that kind of man," Blythe said, rubbing her wrist. "Why are you running him down? You don't know him, either."

"I'm a psychiatrist. I know people."

They crossed the lobby to the elevators. "Oh, you do?" Blythe said. "Well, you don't know him." She stalked onto an open elevator and punched the button for her floor.

"I don't want to know him!" Garth joined her, glaring at her.

"You don't have to! Just don't pretend he's not the yummiest man you ever met! And for your information, that's what Candy sees in him!"

"Yummy? Oh, my God, you women. Yummy doesn't count for anything."

"It sure helps." They'd reached the twenty-third floor and got out. Blythe took off toward the apartment at a near run with Garth right beside her, keeping up without difficulty. She jabbed the key at the door and charged in.

"What matters," Garth persisted, "is financial security and steadiness and dependability. Look at the guy. What kind of money does he make writing political columns? And there he was, acting like a big shot, paying the bill for dinner. Besides that, he's already proved he's totally undependable, and Candy's had enough undependable people in her life."

"How was he undependable?" Blythe demanded to know.

"He stood Candy up. He took up with the first other woman he met. You."

"For heaven's sake! He thought I *was*... Oh, forget it," Blythe said disgustedly. The man had gone insane.

"I wish I could," Garth snapped. "I'm afraid it's too late for me to get a hotel room," he said coldly. "The airports are just now opening again and every hotel in town is packed. If I may have your permission to spend the night on your sofa, I'll leave tomorrow."

"I insist you take my room," she said just as coldly. "I'll sleep on the sofa."

"Don't be silly."

"I'm not being silly. I'm being a good hostess," she said through her teeth. "I intend to take the sofa." *I intend to see Candy the minute she comes in and assess the damage.* "Just give me a minute to get some clothes and a toothbrush." She dashed in and darted around furiously for a few minutes, then emerged clutching the first outfit that had caught her eye. "I'll be gone by the time you wake up in the morning."

"Fine," he said, went to her room and slammed the door.

For some reason, that made her maddest of all. She went directly to the door and opened it without knocking. "And another thing," she said. "Candy sure has you figured out wrong. She was yelling at you this morning for not being able to express your anger. I think you know how to express it just fine." Then she slammed the door.

It opened at once. "There are a lot of things Candy doesn't know about me," he said, practically snarling, and then, to Blythe's irritation, got the last slam.

Yes, Garth knew how to express his anger, but what exactly was he mad about? Exhausted from the tension, she went into Candy's room long enough to get into the most unrevealing nightgown she owned—a flannel granny gown that was going to be much too warm—stretched out on the sofa under a pink mohair throw and closed her eyes.

Behind her eyelids, Max and Candy were locked in a passionate embrace. Her eyes flew open. Surely not. Surely Max was just as sad not to be with her as she was not to be with him.

She closed her eyes again, and there they were, still at it. She moaned.

Thirty sleepless minutes later, she decided cocoa might be a good idea. Quiet as a cat, she got up and went to the kitchen to warm some milk. She was measuring cocoa into a mug when the phone rang. It took her a couple of rings to put down the mug and the measuring spoon and wipe the stray cocoa off her fingers. She'd just pushed the Talk button when the ringing stopped.

Either the caller had changed his mind or Garth had answered the phone. She waited for him to yell at her to pick up, but nothing happened. She stood there staring at the phone, her nerves stretched to the limit, until the unmistakable scent of scorched milk sent her flying to the stove to start over on the cocoa.

As if the day hadn't been bad enough, Candy didn't come home.

THE MINUTE MAX STEPPED into his apartment with Candy, he got mad at Tiger Templeton and his sidekick Poky of Smooth Moves all over again for not being close enough to the city to deliver his furniture this afternoon.

Mad at Bloomingdale's, too, because they *had* delivered the two pieces of furniture he'd bought online—a soft, deep sofa and an even softer, deeper mattress and box spring with a frame.

King-size.

Six down pillows and a huge down comforter. An apartment ready for foreplay, then sex, nothing else.

Plus, Bloomingdale's had graciously made up the bed with the sheets he'd ordered because his mother had said they were the best, and he'd ordered them in black, knowing he wasn't all that expert at doing laundry. A fact Candy was even now discovering—the sheets, not the part about his mother—because she was exploring every inch of his stripped-down seduction cell.

"Ooh, four-hundred-count pima cotton," she was cooing from the bedroom while he still stood woodenly at the door. "Black! I see a zebra-striped duvet cover to go with them. And a zebra rug on the floor."

She was suddenly beside him. "Zebra stripes turn—" she moved up closer "—me—" she put her perfect pink mouth to his ear "—on."

His eardrum popped.

"So you enjoy decorating." It was the only non-provocative thing he could think of to say.

She backed away an inch. "Hell, no. That's Blythe's department. I just..." Uh-oh, she was making her move again. "...have hot sexual fantasies involving zebra stripes."

"How about a brandy?" He wheeled into the kitchen. "Can't make coffee yet, but I do have brandy." A cyanide pill, that was what he wished he'd thought to buy at the drugstore. He peeked around the corner of the kitchen door. Candy had stretched herself out on his sofa. Hot pink toenails grabbed his attention and led it to her endless, perfect legs, which eventually reached the hemline of her alarmingly short skirt.

Most guys would find the view irresistible. As for him, he was grateful she hadn't stretched out facing him. His interest and curiosity lay entirely in what was going on across town between Blythe and Garth.

As soon as he'd heard Garth was sleeping at Candy's and Blythe's, he'd wanted to invite Garth to stay with him. Invite, then sling the guy over his shoulder and carry him here where he could keep an eye on him and Garth could protect him from Candy, but he couldn't exactly invite him to a nearly empty apartment. Besides, he'd only packed one set of towels in his duffel bag.

He poured the expensive brandy into cheap paper drugstore cups and carried the drinks into the living room, telling himself that as smart, sensible and clear-headed as he was, he'd think of an escape hatch in a minute. Candy patted the sofa beside her. Since she was lying diagonally on it, sitting beside her would have meant lying down beside her, so he went to the opposite end of the sofa and sat down beside her feet.

Candy accepted this and the cup of brandy with a patient smile. "This is a great apartment," she said. "I wouldn't have figured you for a prewar place. I was thinking Trump Towers, something modern and sleek."

"I like old," he said.

"In apartments only," she said, giving him a slant-eyed sideways glance. "You like new beds, new sofas, new women…"

"How do you like working at the *Telegraph?*" he said abruptly.

"Love it. Especially now." She batted her eyelashes.

"Big story in the works?"

"Big man in the works." She slithered her thighs together and slid a footful of hot pink toes toward his butt.

God, this was boring. As he tried to think of something to say that she couldn't twist into a come-on, an idea came to him. "I'm thirsty," he said. "I don't have much, but I do have water." He rolled up off the sofa a split second before her toes slid under him and went back to the kitchen. He had Perrier and a single lime he'd picked up from a sidewalk vendor. Citrus was a great diuretic. He put a third of the lime into her paper cup of sparkling water and returned to the fencing match.

An hour later, it became clear to him that the woman had the bladder of a buffalo. All he wanted was to get her out of the room for a couple of minutes, and the powder room was a logical place she might go willingly. So he'd gotten almost a quart of Perrier into her, plus the juice of a lime, plus three brandies. The brandy seemed to have no effect on her, and she still didn't have to go to the bathroom.

She had him pinned to his end of the sofa with her body wrapped around him while he carried on a unilateral conversation. Now he decided to take it in a new direction. He'd rely on the power of suggestion. "What I like about living in an apartment," he said, "is not having to do yard work. I remember my dad out in the yard every summer night, pointing the hose at the flower beds, the water gushing out in a high arc like he was, well, you know."

"We had a gardener," Candy said, and stuck her tongue in his ear.

"My dad would have loved that," he said next. "Mom would have, too. Sometimes they had to run the sprinkler system all day, and she'd go crazy hearing the sound of water running all day long, day in, day out."

Candy wiggled around until she got one breast stuck right into his armpit.

"And that's sort of weird, because the sound of running water is supposed to be soothing," he rambled on, feeling the pressure in his own body build up to an intolerable level, and he'd only had one brandy. "That's why people have all these fountains, or grottos, with the water running down rocks or whatever, drip, drip, drip, because it— Would you excuse me a minute?" He extricated himself from Candy and quick-stepped to the bathroom off his bedroom. He made it just in time.

A bulb lit up in his head. His cell phone was in his pocket. He hadn't needed to get Candy out of the room. He'd only needed to leave the room himself. Smart. Sensible. Clearheaded. Sure he was. He whipped the phone out and dialed the one local number he knew by heart.

Bart Klemp's depressed-sounding voice was like a show-stopper tune to his ears. "Bart, call my cell phone," he said rapidly. "Just call. I'll do the rest." He pushed the End button and returned to Candy.

"A touch more brandy?" he asked her while he was still safely standing, and then his pants pocket began to vibrate. "Sorry," he apologized, and dug out the cell phone.

"Shoot," Candy said. "I thought we were about to get kinky."

"It's me," Bart said. "Use me as you will."

"Mom," Max said. "Hi! Mom, are you crying? What's wrong?"

"I tried to warn you," Bart moaned. "I told you she'd jump you."

Max turned toward Candy so she wouldn't miss a thing and drew his brows together in what he hoped resembled a desperately worried frown. "Oh, no. You think it might be a heart attack?"

"Damn good reporter, though," Bart ruminated. "Even a nympho can be a good reporter. Don't think she's a nympho, though. Just think..." He trailed off.

"Think what?" Max said before he could stop himself. "I mean, you think I should come right now?"

"Think she likes men," Bart said. "Needs male attention, that is. One of those things that starts up in childhood and you have to go to a shrink to figure out why you—"

"Try to calm down, Mom," Max said earnestly. "I'll be on the next train."

"You'll be safer there," Bart said.

Max hung up. "My dad," he said in a heartbroken voice. "Mom says it might be a heart attack."

"I'm sorry," Candy said, and it made him feel bad that she actually did sound sorry.

"So I guess we'll have to call it a night, because I have to leave," Max said, making his tone a little firmer.

"I guess we will," Candy agreed. "Your mother needs you." But she didn't move from the sofa.

"I can take you home and then go to Penn Station," Max said pointedly, pulling his sport coat back over his dress shirt and suit pants.

"I can't go home," Candy said, widening her already

big blue eyes. "I don't want to disturb Blythe and Garth."

Red flashes of jealous rage stung Max's eyeballs. "Then where would you like to go?" he said.

"I'll just stay here," she said. "Call me. I want to know how your dad is."

He'd lost the battle. Growling to himself, he stalked out the door, jogged to the elevator, got his phone out, raised the antenna, reached the first floor and ran out into the night. Just around the corner, he dialed Blythe and Candy's apartment. It rang once, twice, and then a man's voice answered. Garth's voice.

And the way he answered told Max everything he needed to know. He hung up, heartsick.

He couldn't believe it. He thought he'd figured Blythe out in one glorious night. A hot and sexy lady, but a monogamous one. He wasn't thinking true love everlasting—much too soon to do that—but he couldn't imagine her going straight from him to Garth without giving it a second thought.

Just showed you how wrong you could be.

More disappointed than he thought the situation warranted—*get a grip, man, it was just one accidental night*—he kept pacing south. The Mayflower Hotel had an available room. He checked in and climbed naked between the sheets to contemplate the fickleness of women.

BLYTHE WAS AT HER DESK in her tiny cubicle at seven o'clock on Saturday morning, wearing the outfit she'd selected the night before. The ivory silk pants and shirt had needed pressing then, and needed it worse now. She'd hoped the humidity would shake out the wrinkles, but it hadn't. It had just made her hair frizzier.

She'd cleared her desk and was reorganizing her paper clip drawer while she waited for her next assignment when Candy's long shadow darkened her doorway. Candy was holding a disk in her hand.

"Bart says you should look this over and fine-tune it," she said, giving Blythe a slow, wide smile. The smile of a sated woman.

"You know, you don't have to come bearing disks," Blythe said crisply. "We are networked here. You can e-mail the story to me and I can send it back."

"But I wanted to see you." More of the slow smile, with a sigh added on.

Blythe was determined to hide the hurt she felt inside. "Did you have a nice time with Max?" she asked, trying to keep her voice neutral while she wrenched the disk out of Candy's grasp and shoved it into her A-drive.

"Frigging wonderful," Candy breathed.

Blythe couldn't help herself. She needed confirmation to be as upset as she wanted to be. "You spent the night in his bed," she said.

Candy hesitated a second, then her smile widened. "Yes," she said. "I spent the night in his bed."

"Congratulations," Blythe said, and attacked Candy's story. She could barely see the monitor through the tears that began to fill her eyes. How could he? How could he make love to Candy so soon after the most wonderful night she, Blythe, had ever had? Most men, she knew from experience, were all plumbing, no heart, except for Sven, who had neither. She'd thought Max was different. How stupid of her.

Bart stuck his head through the cubicle doorway. "Anybody hear how Max's dad is?" he said.

"How'd you know about Max's dad?" Candy snapped.

"How'd you know we knew Max?" Blythe chimed in. This seemed the most interesting question to her. She had no idea what Bart meant about Max's dad.

"I know everything," Bart said in his usual depressed moan. "Max's folks are old friends of mine. His mother called me. I thought he might have shared a little detail like his dad having a heart attack. What I really want to know is will he be in today?" Again, for Bart, a long speech. A speech Blythe was finding very interesting.

"I haven't heard from him yet this morning," Candy said. She seemed to be stumbling a little over the words.

"Why didn't you tell me?" Blythe said. She wouldn't recognize Max's dad if he were floating in her soup, but she still felt terribly sad for Max. And sad about Max. And mad at Max for falling straight into bed with Candy after his night with her, even if his father *had* had a heart attack and she ought to be feeling sympathetic.

"Is it a party?" Max said suddenly from somewhere behind Bart.

"There's no more room in here," Blythe snapped. "Gather somewhere else to chat. I have a job to do."

The cubicle fell into silence. Blythe reddened, realizing she'd been rude not only to the two people she was maddest at but to her boss, as well. Max backed out of the cubicle. Bart backed out and stood in front of Max. Candy backed out and went straight to Max's side. Blythe could still see, and hear, all three of them through the doorway while she pretended to be unvitalizing Candy's follow-up story on the drug take-down in the Bronx, which had been a fiasco due to the power outage. Nobody important showed up. Even drug dealers needed transportation.

"How's your dad?" Candy said, keeping a barely professional distance between herself and Max, merely touching his arm in a supportive way while she spoke directly to his cheek.

"You're here and not in Jersey," Bart said. "He must be okay."

"False alarm," Max said.

Bells were going off in the left side of Blythe's brain. "You've been to Jersey and back since when?" she called out.

They all went silent again. She bit her lip.

"Since soon after I got home last night," Max said, giving each word emphasis as he glowered at her.

Blythe dragged her gaze away from him and settled it on Candy. They couldn't have had a whole lot of hot sex then, could they? Not if Max had been to somewhere as yet undisclosed in New Jersey and back. It might not have been a mere Path train trip to Hoboken. It might have been a long, long New Jersey Transit journey to some town near the border.

Was that what he was trying to tell her? Was that why Candy was looking irritated, when she should have been telling Max how happy she was that his father was all right?

Blythe could feel her heart softening. Maybe she hadn't lost Max to Candy's universal appeal. But if she hadn't, why did he look so mad at her?

"Come talk to me," Bart said to Max.

"Sure," Max said. With one last furious look at Blythe, he stalked away behind Bart.

Candy said hastily, "So, like you said, you can just e-mail the story back to me..."

"Come back in here right now," Blythe said, trying to glower just like Max.

Candy halted, then slowly joined Blythe in the cubicle. "What's wrong?" she said. "You need some eyedrops? You look all squinty."

Blythe dropped her attempt to glower. "No, I just want to know if you deliberately left me with a misimpression of your 'wonderful night' with Max."

Candy bristled. "As if that's any of your frigging business."

"Your not being honest with me is my business," Blythe said firmly. She was utterly amazed at her own temerity. For once, she must really care, care enough to stand up to Candy. That was a whole lot of caring.

Candy pouted. "Well, you asked me if I spent the night in his bed, and I did."

"Because he was in New Jersey." Her heart felt so light all of a sudden that she wanted to get up and do a dance.

"Right. But he's interested, Blythe," Candy said with a quick return to earnestness. "Tonight will be different."

"Tonight?" Blythe's voice faltered. "You have a date with him tonight?"

"Yes," Candy said, looking satisfied. "He doesn't know it yet, but we are definitely going out together again tonight."

"Candy," Blythe said, "this *frigging* story of yours is pure crap. Go away and leave me alone and I'll see what I can do with it."

Candy's eyes widened. "What *is* wrong with you?"

she said in a startled whisper. "You're not acting like yourself."

"I'm acting like a woman who spent the night with Garth in her bed," Blythe said. "That says it all, really, doesn't it?"

6

"YOU JUST GOT HERE and you're already having woman problems," Bart said when he'd settled down with Max in his office.

Max recognized the head-shaking and the world's-coming-to-an-end attitude as being pure Bart. He leaned back in the visitor's chair and crossed his right foot over his left knee, feeling the weight of women and frustration and frustrating women lift from his shoulders in the presence of someone he'd known and trusted all his life. "I was thinking the same thing," he admitted. "This is the fastest I've ever worked."

"You've been like this since you were a little kid," Bart said. "Never could say no to anybody."

"That's a direct quote from my dad," Max said, frowning.

"We talk," Bart said.

"Wish you'd talk about something besides me," Max said.

"We do. You barely get a mention."

"But you're right," Max said. "First thing I shouldn't have done was accept a blind date so Candy's feelings wouldn't be hurt. Ha," he added as an aside. "I'd like to see somebody hurt her feelings without getting killed. Anyway, next thing I shouldn't have done was get in that damned elevator, but how was I supposed to know there'd be a blackout? And the third thing I shouldn't have done was get the hots for Blythe until I'd scoped out the situation, but I didn't want to hurt *her* feelings by turning her down. If you could have seen her, heard her," he said, leaning forward to emphasize his point, "you'd understand. She was so sweet and innocent about the whole thing. How could I have—"

"Yeah, yeah," Bart said.

So Max leaned back and went on. "Third thing I *should* have done was tell Candy where to get off." This time when he leaned forward it was irritation that energized him. "Do you realize those two think they can decide who gets me? Like I'm a...a cucumber?" He noticed Bart was looking a little stunned.

"I'm not following a whole lot of this," Bart said.

Max sighed. "Don't try. It's too depressing."

"Want to stay with Linda and me until it blows over?" Bart said. "Now that the kids are gone, we kind of rattle around that big old place up in Riverdale."

The full weight of his worries settled back down on him, and Max's jaw clenched. "No, I'd rather have Garth stay with you and Linda until it blows over."

"Who's Garth? I mean, any friend of yours is welcome in our—"

"Believe me, he's no friend. He's the guy who's supposed to get Blythe. Candy's decided they're made for each other," Max burst out. "What a crock. Imagine, a couple named Garth-th-th and Blythe-th-th. Their friends would all be thongue-thied."

Bart stared at him silently. "Maybe you'd better tell me what's going on. Tell it in some kind of order the average brain can handle."

So Max did. It took quite a while.

"You got big problems," Bart said when he'd finally

wound down. "Think you can do a little work with all these big problems hanging around your neck?"

Max straightened in his chair. "Of course," he said. "Work is my first priority. I've already done a lot of research into the City Council scandal. Now I need to get out into the field, get the lowdown on these guys. Oh," he added as a stray thought distracted him. "Think you could find Candy some night jobs?"

Because he was suddenly seeing how being honest with Candy, saying no to her, could be the *kindest* thing to do. He must really want to see more of Blythe. She hadn't gone to bed with Garth last night. He knew it in the depths of his soul, whatever the circumstantial evidence might be. So…he'd just ask her. Right now.

"At least I know you're your dad's kid," he heard Bart saying as he strode purposefully out of his office. "You'll get to work one of these days."

WHEN BLYTHE PICKED UP her phone and a voice said, "So, can you explain yourself?" she knew at once it was Max's voice.

"Where would you like me to start?" Even the coolness in his voice couldn't stop her heart from pounding, couldn't stop the moisture she felt between her thighs. She wanted to hug the phone between her breasts, but it would have made talking difficult.

"Start at about ten o'clock last night. Candy told me you said—in your own words, she said—that Garth slept in your bed last night."

The *Telegraph's* prized new hire had become incoherent. Blythe hoped that was a good sign, because she was feeling pretty incoherent herself. "That's Candy's little joke of the day," she explained patiently.

"What's funny about it?" His voice rose.

"I don't know, but Candy thinks it's hilarious. She told me she slept in your bed last night."

"And you believed her?" Now he was roaring. Did he know half the sixth floor, Editorial, Features and Sports, was hearing every word he said? "What kind of person do you think I am?"

"At the time," Blythe explained, "I thought you were the kind of person you think I am, the kind of person neither of us had previously thought the other one was." She was definitely incoherent, but then, the situation didn't make much sense, either, and furthermore, Max seemed to understand her as well as she'd understood him. With any luck at all, they might one day ride off together, babbling into the sunset.

"I called you last night after I escaped from Candy." He paused, and Blythe could hear him taking a deep breath. She steeled herself for whatever decibel level he was capable of, which she imagined was pretty high, and she was right.

"And Garth answered! You were right there. You heard what he said—'Blythe's bed.'"

"He did?"

"Sounded pretty straightforward to me!"

"Where are you, Max?" Blythe said. One increment louder and her floor would be able to hear him, too.

"I'm at home, hoping the slowest moving van in the world will show up, and trying to write a column."

At least he'd lowered his voice a little. At least he wasn't upstairs on the sixth floor destroying her reputation. "Garth got to the phone before I did," she said.

"Because he was on the phone side of your bed!"

Uh-oh, the tone was up again. "I wasn't in bed. I slept on the sofa."

There was a long silence. Then Max said, "And Garth slept in your bed."

"Just as I told Candy. As a joke. Because she told me she'd slept in your bed. Which upset me pretty badly until I figured out it was a joke when Bart came in to ask about your father's condition." She hesitated. "Did your father actually have a condition to inquire about?"

"No. That's how I escaped. Bart helped me." Another long silence ensued. "You didn't trust me," Max finally muttered.

"Of course not," she assured him. "I mean, if you think about it, we didn't even have a proper introduction until yesterday morning. I don't know the first thing about you."

"Yes, you do."

She could sense his mood lightening. All the sensations his voice caused in her intensified. She was melting right there in her chair. "Well, yes, I guess I do know the first thing about you, but it's not usually the first thing a person gets to know."

And at last she heard a touch of laughter in his voice. "Want to know more?"

Oh, yes. "I..." Her voice faltered. "I can't. I promised."

"Forget your stupid promise. Candy had her chance and she blew it. I don't want to go out with her. I want to go out with you." He paused, and his voice took on a new tone, low and rhythmic. "No, I take that back. I don't want to go out with you. What I want to do with you..."

Blythe's pulse throbbed. She locked her trembling knees tightly together beneath her desk.

"I want to unbutton your blouse with my teeth. I

want to sink my face between your beautiful little round breasts and then tickle them with my tongue while I peel the rest of your clothes off and do a lot more things with my tongue. Doesn't that sound like fun, Blythe? Can you sit there and tell me you don't want me as much as I want you? I wasn't up to form Thursday night. I mean, the elevator thing, and all those stairs. I can do better. Don't you want to find out how much better I can do?" He added the clincher. "You're telling me you don't want me enough to risk making a friend mad?"

That was the point, really, wasn't it? Did she want Max enough to risk losing Candy's friendship, her support? Did Candy deserve to have her many kindnesses paid back this way? She'd known Candy, her good side and her bad side, for years. She'd barely met Max, although what she knew about him she really, really liked, oh, more than liked, wanted, had been obsessing over since the minute he stumbled into her life. She wriggled desperately in her chair. "It's not that I don't want to, but I...I can't."

"Why the hell not?" His shout was deafening.

She jumped. "Because I promised."

"Why do you let her bully you? Does she have something on you? Is she blackmailing you?"

"No, no. Candy doesn't bully me. She's really a good person inside, Max." Now she was almost pleading with him, and not in her own best interests. "It's just that, well, I stole you away from her, quite accidentally—"

"Listen up." Uh-oh, he was shouting again. "I'm not a toy you can give Candy for her damned birthday. I don't belong to her! You didn't steal me! This is insane!"

It was, actually, now that Blythe thought about it, but she'd made that promise.

"Don't make an issue of it just yet, okay?" she said, still pleading. "Go out with Candy tonight."

"Leaving you alone with Garth? I want that man out of your apartment! If the damned moving van ever gets here with another set of towels, I'll force him to stay with me. How long's his damned conference, anyway?"

"Through Sunday. But he and I had a—"

"Someone is knocking on my door," Max said ominously before she could tell him about the really peculiar fight Garth had picked with her. "Hang on. Maybe it's the movers."

Blythe hung on, hoping she'd get to tell him about the fight. The next thing she heard in the background was, "Candy. What a surprise," and Candy's laughing voice saying, "I brought lunch. And wait until you see what I've got for dessert."

Then Max's voice on the phone again, cold and flat. "Thank you for your time, Councilman. Maybe we can chat again later this afternoon." He hung up.

Blythe felt as cold and flat as his voice. As she turned dully back to her work, she noticed an e-mail icon that had popped up on the monitor while she and Max were talking. It was from Candy. "See what you can do with this, okay, sweetie?" was the note that accompanied the attachment. A story Candy had written in careless haste for Blythe to turn into something publishable, just before she went flying off to wreak her wiles on Max.

And she would win. Candy always won. It wasn't fair, not any of it. Blythe felt she'd finally reached bottom. There was only one way to go—back up toward the sun.

First, of course, she'd fix Candy's story.

MAX WAS GETTING BETTER at fighting off women than he'd ever thought he'd have to get. It took considerable skill, since his apartment was really just two big, high-ceilinged rooms plus a kitchen and bathroom. At one point during Candy's hot pursuit he was afraid he might have to try scaling a wall. Even as he congratulated himself, he wondered why he couldn't just say, "Go home, Candy. It's your roommate I want and I guess I'm just a one-at-a-time guy."

Like my dad.

Maybe he was more like his father than he realized.

Or maybe it was because Blythe seemed to care so much about keeping her promise to Candy.

If the moving van had come, which it didn't, it would have saved him.

The cable guy did, although Max's flat-screen set wasn't there to hook up, so Max wouldn't know whether he actually had service or not. At least he managed to convince Candy it was an important issue, and that it was important for her to stay there with the guy to keep him from going on to another job.

It was no trouble at all to convince the cable serviceman to hang around, drooling over Candy, while Max went over to Broadway to the closest, undoubtedly most expensive electronics store in Manhattan, and bought a smaller set than the one on the moving van. He'd like having it in the bedroom anyway. He could afford it, and his credit card company knew he could afford it or it wouldn't have given him such an exclusive card and granted him virtually unlimited spending.

Still, spending wildly went against the grain, but he was desperate. While he waited for the salesman to run the card through and find a clerk with a dolly to walk Max and his new television set home, he called Bart and begged for deliverance.

"You have to cover a story?" he said to Candy when he got home and she sulkily informed him Bart was sending her out to Staten Island. "Aw."

"I'll be back by eight," Candy said. "Maybe earlier. Pick me up at the office. We'll start out at a party a friend of mine is giving. Then—" she batted her eyelashes at him "—who knows what we might think of next?"

"I'm having drinks with a city councilman close to your apartment," he countered. "I'll pick you up at home."

"Where?" Candy said, fixing a gaze on him that was like two artificial ice cubes. "Where are you meeting him?"

"The Mark," Max said. A good journalist did his research. The hotel was close to Blythe's apartment. Or Candy's, depending on your focus.

"Which councilman?"

Max frowned. "I'm not at liberty to say."

"The same councilman you were talking to when I got here?"

"Yes."

"You sounded very vague with him then. When did you firm up the appointment?"

"He called me on my cell while I was out buying the television set." This woman would make an awesome wife. Or probation officer.

"When are you meeting him?"

Not all good journalists could do math, but Max was, at the moment, highly motivated. "Six-thirty," he said. "I shouldn't have any problem making it to your apartment by eight o'clock."

"Well, okay," Candy said. "Garth will have talked Blythe into going out to dinner by then, or not going out at all," she added with a wicked smile, "so if you beat me home, just wait in the lobby."

"Sure thing," Max said through his teeth.

She reached for him.

"Your story," he said. "Staten Island. You'd better hurry."

BLYTHE LEFT THE OFFICE at five o'clock. She was neatening and cleaning bathrooms in a distracted sort of way when the phone rang. She didn't want it to be Max, and still somehow, at the same time she was dying for it to be Max. She snatched up the receiver, understandably alarmed to hear a high-pitched scream. "Blythe, I've got the most incredible news!"

It was Sacha Halliday, a friend of hers and Candy's. Blythe tried hard to rise to whatever the occasion was. "Which is?"

"I sold my book!"

"Oh, Sacha, I'm thrilled for you," Blythe said, and meant it.

Sacha bubbled for a while, things about advances and revisions and sequels and prequels, agents and editors and contracts and promotions, while Blythe listened patiently, trying to share the joy. "And the reason I called," Sacha said at last, "is that I'm giving myself an impromptu party tonight. Is that too vain or what?" She giggled. "I already reached Candy at the office. She won't promise. Seems she's got a hot new fella.''

Not yet she doesn't. Blythe was startled by how catty she was feeling. "Yes, she—"

"I told her to bring him and let us get a look at him." Sacha paused, then said in a conspirator's hiss, "She said you did, too, and probably wouldn't want to come, but I'm calling you anyway."

Even more startling was the rage that climbed Blythe's throat and moved hotly to her face. Her scalp prickled. Perspiration broke out on her forehead and her face. Candy was refusing invitations for her now? Because...

Candy wanted to take Max to Sacha's party, leaving Blythe to star in *Home Alone With Garth.*

The words *Escape From Garth* appeared in her mind. In neon scarlet, but that was because she was seeing red. "Candy's trying to fix me up with an old friend of hers," she told Sacha. "It's not working, but Candy won't give up on it." She'd regained enough control not to dump the whole story on Sacha, this being the novelist's moment of glory. "I'd love to come to your victory party," she said, "and I'll be coming alone."

"Anytime after seven-thirty," Sacha bubbled. "God knows what we'll have to eat, but there will be plenty to drink, I promise."

Blythe spent ten minutes slipping into a short, snug black dress and a frantic thirty minutes assembling a triple batch of Canellini and Italian tuna fish with garlic, onion, parsley and olive oil. It was a rich, filling spread almost everybody liked, and she always kept the ingredients on hand. She'd take it along to the party and pick up mini pitas on her way. Garth still wasn't home. This had to be her lucky day. She tossed

Max's pretzels and mixed nuts into her tote bag and stepped into the hallway.

"Blythe," Garth said from ten feet down the hallway, "you're leaving? Candy said we should have dinner together tonight."

She almost dropped the tote bag. "I can't have dinner," she said, calming down enough to release the creative liar within. "I'm taking...food...to a...to a wake," she said. "A proper Irish wake."

"Oh-h," he said, quickly sympathetic and very, very nice. "Who died?"

"A...sister of my foster mother's who conveniently relocated to, um, Brooklyn," she improvised. "I know, I know," she said, throwing up one hand to forestall a virtually certain inquisition from Garth about the stress of being orphaned, which Candy must have told him about. "It's hard. It's painful. It's...life." She delivered him a sad smile she hoped was tinged with the wisdom of ages, then fled for the elevator, hearing behind her his insistent suggestion that he would go with her, see her through the wake, and they'd have dinner after.

IT WAS SIX O'CLOCK and the moving van hadn't arrived. While Max paced his two rooms—plus kitchen and bath—the Smooth Moves driver called. "You're here," Max cried out like a child at Christmas.

"Nope," Tiger Templeton said instead of, "You bet." "Mrs. Edwards kept changing her mind about where she wanted the furniture, and we had to spend the night in Cincy. I'm in upstate New York dropping off a load of antiques to a dealer. If that goes okay, I'll see you tomorrow for sure."

Max hung up, feeling thoughtful. Antiques, that's

what he needed to get him through this phase with Candy. Hard chairs, slippery Victorian sofas, a bed that squeaked.

But for now, all he wanted was to catch Blythe alone. His plan was to head to the apartment early, before Garth got home. Surely he had conference cocktail parties to go to. Max knew what conferences were like.

So after a swift call to the actual councilman who was next on his list to interview, and who proved gratifyingly willing to talk, he hightailed it over to the east side of town.

He announced himself to the doorman, who buzzed the apartment and apparently got a "go" sign to send him right up, so up he went. Filled with passion and purpose, he waited with desperate anticipation for the apartment door to open, and when it did, the person he was looking at was Garth.

"Langston," Garth said. "Hello."

"Laughton," Max said. "Hello to you, too." Deeply disappointed to be talking to Garth instead of Blythe, he added, "Candy's not expecting me until eight, but I got through a little early. Is she here?"

"No," Garth said. "But if you're picking her up, I know she'll be here by eight."

So where the hell was Blythe? He couldn't ask, not directly, anyway. "I thought you and Blythe would be on your way to dinner. Or something."

"She had to go to a wake," Garth said, assuming a lugubrious expression. "Her foster aunt died."

"Really?" Max said, smiling.

"Laughton," Garth said, "the woman died. Blythe has suffered a loss."

Max smoothed his face. "Sorry," he said. "I have a nervous tic. Happens at the worst times. So Blythe has gone to a wake. Is it out of town somewhere? Will she have to be away for a while?"

"I don't think so," Garth said. He sounded glum. "The wake's in Brooklyn."

"Where in Brooklyn? Is it safe for her to go there by herself?"

Garth gave him such a puzzled look that Max had to remind himself that the strong feelings he had for Blythe were based on nothing more than one unforgettable night. What was it about her that had made her get under his skin so fast?

He could only think of one thing, and it was so Freudian, he wasn't going to let himself think about it.

"Well, look, let's sit down and have a drink while you wait for Candy," Garth said. He wandered off to the kitchen in an aimless way that was very unlike the man Max had met yesterday. "Scotch, right?" he called out, but he still sounded listless. "I can't figure out what's going on here. So are you sleeping with Candy now? Did the girls come to some kind of agreement about it?"

"You could get decked for calling them girls," Max joined Garth in the kitchen and leaned against a counter. "I'm going to explain something to you, Brandon. They don't seem to understand it. Maybe you will. They don't get to..." About to go into his spiel, the image of Blythe's face pleading with him to go out with Candy, give Candy a chance, stopped him short. He forced a grin. "They don't get to tell me what's what," he said with macho bravado. Pounding his chest, he guessed, would be going too far. "So, yeah, Blythe was a mistake and now I'm dating Candy."

"And sleeping with her."

Max heard an odd note in Garth's voice. He hoped it

was envy because he imagined Max to be having hot, wet sex with Candy while he wasn't getting any from Blythe. He decided to give the guy a break. "Not yet," he said. "These things take time."

"Not with Candy they don't." Garth's voice was really flat now. Max could have made a coat rack in the time it was taking the man to make a Scotch and water.

"Oh, she puts on a good show," he said offhandedly, "but underneath she's just a nice woman."

"She is, isn't she?" Garth said earnestly. His face lit up. "And here she is."

Candy breezed in through the front door yelling, "Blythe, Garth, has Max—hey, you're already here," she said as she sidled up to Max and put a little more weight on the kitchen counter. "Where's Blythe? Dressing?"

"At a wake," Garth said.

"A foster aunt died," Max said.

"A foster aunt?" Candy said in disbelief. "Where'd that come from?"

"That's what she said," Garth insisted. "She looked like she was taking food."

"Blythe would. Take food, that is," Candy said with a frown. "Oh, well, I thought I knew everything about her, but maybe not." A puzzled look crossed her face, then she turned to Garth. "She left you all alone here?"

"She didn't even ask me if I wanted to go to the wake." His lower lip poked out a little.

"That was terrible of her. So you have to go with Max and me to Sacha's party," Candy said. "It'll be fine," she added when Garth started an unconvincing protest. "Sacha sold her damned book and wants to rub it into as many people as she can cram into her apartment. Just give me a second to freshen up."

She somehow managed to slide her entire left side down Max's entire right side as she slithered away from the counter, out of the kitchen and toward her bedroom, her hips swinging in a pair of extra-tight pants that must have shrunk in the wash.

Max watched her go, then turned to Garth in hopes of getting that Scotch at last, and saw that Garth was watching her go, too.

Hmm.

BLYTHE STOOD AT THE EDGE of a tiny room crammed with people, all of whom were attempting a hit on the solitary bowl of food that sat on a proportionately tiny table in the center of the space. Her tuna and bean spread. Sacha had ordered extravagant amounts of inexpensive wine from the closest liquor store, but had been too excited to do anything about food. Just now Blythe was trying to open the pretzel and mixed-nut cans before Sacha's party guests began to devour one another.

"Do you have any big bowls?" she asked the next time Sacha skipped by.

"What?" Sacha said. Her eyes were glazed, not from alcohol, Blythe knew, but from a success high.

Blythe gave up and slid along the wall around the celebrants until she reached the short stretch of miniature appliances that constituted Sacha's kitchen. A search of the cupboards above netted her an ice bucket and a plastic bowl in a Christmassy design. They'd have to do.

She filled the ice bucket with nuts and the bowl with pretzels, put the nuts down on the nearest table and stood back to keep from being crushed as the crowd turned as one to attack the bowl. She crept to the other side of the room with the pretzels.

It gave her a good feeling to do these things for Sacha. Sacha had been living on a shoestring while she wrote her novel, supporting herself by dog-walking and pet-sitting, so this sale would change her life. This room was Sacha's entire apartment, and it would fit into Blythe's bedroom with space to spare.

Without Candy, Blythe knew she'd be living in an apartment like Sacha's. But Sacha was so happy here, doing what she wanted to do when she wanted to do it, with no one else to answer to—

Blythe was thinking hard about her own choices when the door opened suddenly and Candy swept in, trailed by Max and—oh, no, please not—Garth. He'd know she'd lied to him. She'd be so embarrassed.

Cornered like a wild animal! Her choices were to confess, which would have been her natural choice, or hide.

Hide, definitely.

7

BLYTHE COULD ONLY FIND TWO options for hiding in Sacha's apartment. She could either attach herself to the back of one of the larger men and hope he wouldn't notice, or she could try to make it to Sacha's single armchair.

The armchair was her best bet. Dropping to the floor behind the guests, she crept toward the chair, reached it without being noticed and squatted behind it with her skirt tucked tightly between her thighs and calves.

Amid cries of "Hey, Candy," Candy trilled, "Sacha! I am ecstatic for you."

Blythe envisioned Candy, overdressed and glamorous in silk capris, a black-and-white sequined top and spiked heels, exchanging hugs and air kisses with Sacha in her long rayon sundress and sandals. Then it was Sacha's voice, saying, "This must be..."

Then Candy's, answering, "No, *this* one's Max."

"Oh," Sacha said, "Hi, Max."

"This has to be the greatest day of your life," Blythe heard Max say, his voice so warm and cuddly she could imagine Sacha glowing from the reawakened realization of her success.

"And may I add my heartiest congratulations. I'm Garth Brandon, Candy's friend."

Blythe thought Garth sounded snippy.

"Thanks, Garth. I understand you and Blythe are—Where is Blythe, anyway?"

Blythe held her breath. Sacha was about to blow her cover.

"Did you ask her to the party?" Candy said, sounding surprised. "I thought I told you..." Her words faded into murmurs and giggles.

Blythe peeked warily over the back of the armchair to find Max staring directly at her hiding spot. When their gazes met, his eyes widened and then his brows drew together. It was a message. The message seemed to be, "Sit. Stay," so she ducked again to avoid the crisis as long as possible.

"Blythe had to go to a wake," Garth said.

"Oh, no..." Sacha began.

Blythe sank her head between her knees. It was all over. She faced discovery, humiliation. She'd be cast out from her group of friends, evicted from her apartment. She squeezed her eyes tight and wished for someone to come to her rescue.

MAX TURNED TO SACHA and gave her a hard stare. He didn't know her. He had no idea, if it came to taking sides, whose side she'd take, Candy's or Blythe's. She fell silent midsentence and returned his stare. She looked smart. As a writer, she probably had an awesome imagination. He held his breath.

"Oh, no," she said again. "Poor Blythe. Who died? I didn't think she had any family members left."

"Some aunt I've never heard of," Candy said in a gripy voice. "Or rather a frigging foster aunt. I must say, I've never heard the term 'foster aunt.'"

"If you were expecting her, she should have called you when she had to cancel," Garth said to Sacha.

"Blythe was orphaned at an early age," Candy said kindly while making a subtle shift of position to line herself up beside Garth. "We can't expect her to have the manners we grew up with, Garth."

"The woman was grieving," Max snapped, sliding a foot toward Sacha. "When you're grieving, you're not thinking about canceling out on a damned party! No offense, Sacha," he said hastily. "This is a wonderful occasion, and I'm sure Blythe would have—"

"Of course she wouldn't think to call me," Sacha protested while lining herself up beside Max. "Bless her heart, I wouldn't have expected her to."

Now Max and Sacha were facing the door while Candy and Garth had their backs to it. Max hoped Blythe was paying attention, because this was her chance.

"I guess I *was* being snobbish," Garth said. "I shouldn't have criticized her manners."

Max would have enjoyed removing a few teeth from his patronizing smile if his attention hadn't been focused on the small black-clad figure creeping on hands and knees toward the door. Instead of snarling at Garth, he felt a smile rising to his face. Blythe's rear end was so cute wriggling along like that. "I'm sure Blythe was disappointed not to be here with you," he said genially.

"When she gets home, you can console her in her grief," Candy said to Garth.

"How about a glass of wine?" Sacha said abruptly.

"Sounds great," Max said. Sacha must have seen Blythe sneaking out, too.

"Don't move," Sacha said. "I'll be back in a second." As Candy started to turn around, Sacha said, "White or red, Candy?"

"White, I guess," Candy said, reversing directions. "Do you have something dry and cold in a chardonnay?"

"Come with me," Sacha said. "You can choose between the box and the jug."

Max saw the door open, and Blythe's rear end vanished through it before it closed again. Garth was making a move on the mixed nuts. Personally, Max saw this as a window of opportunity to make a move on Blythe.

With Candy already drawing a crowd at the wine table and Garth picking through the nuts, probably going for the cashews, and Max a stranger to everyone else in the room, he made it out the door without anyone noticing. Down a long, dreary hall, he saw Blythe waiting at the elevator.

He slowed, giving himself the pleasure of simply looking at her in the little black dress. No more than a slip, really, and it hugged every curve.

If he closed his eyes, he could remember exactly how those curves had felt in his hands.

If he closed his eyes, she'd be on the elevator and out of there while he daydreamed. He quickened his step, moving silently, and sneaked up behind her. "You're not escaping from me," he whispered into her ear.

She jumped and shivered in his arms, then began to struggle. "Go back to the party," she said, sounding panicked. "What if Candy catches you?"

He started to tell her exactly how little he cared if Candy caught them, but realized he had a much better use for their few stolen minutes. Gently, he turned her toward him and bent his head way, way down to kiss her.

SHE FELT THE WARM, SOFT touch of his mouth on hers, felt his arms slide around her, and all her frustrations and worries faded away. Lost in his kiss, she gave him all the sweetness she felt in her heart. His mouth melded with hers, her breasts found the heat of his chest. His hands stroked her back, moving lower and lower until at last she was pressed tight against the hardness of his arousal.

The elevator came and he backed her into it, not breaking the rhythm of his hands or the passion in his kiss.

"We're going up," she murmured against his lips.

"Both of us?"

His fingertips were at the hem of her skirt, tugging it up to her hips, her waist, and then she felt the full power of him through the thin silk of her panties. She moaned. He reached out to push the elevator button again, and it began its descent as an aching heat rose inside her. She writhed against him, felt the tension in his body, knew he was struggling for control while all she could think of doing was letting herself go.

His hands slipped down through the waistband of her panties to rake her bare flesh. She writhed against him, and with a growl of impatience, he lifted her and she wrapped her legs around him, bucking against him, clawing his back with her fingernails as her need grew to unbearable heights. The elevator went up, went down, went up again as she sought his heat, sought the contact of his arousal with the most sensitive, aching part of her. It was suddenly all too much to take. A little cry of surprise burst from her as she exploded, wave after wave of spasms rocking her while he held her tight against him. Damp with perspiration, her hair sticking to her face and tangling with her eye-lashes, she finally stilled, clinging desperately to him.

He pushed the elevator button, still holding her tight, stroking her, burying his face in her breasts. "Damn it, Blythe, how can you feel this way and still go on with your stupid charade?" he groaned.

The elevator slowed. She didn't know how long they'd been on it, but she sensed they hadn't gone down far enough to reach the first floor. They broke apart wildly, Blythe trying to adjust everything at once—her underwear, her skirt, smoothing back her hair. The door opened. Garth and Candy stood outside, gazing in. Blythe wanted to sink through the elevator floor and straight down the shaft.

"The wake is over," Max said calmly. "Blythe managed to make it after all. Lucky for you, Garth." Blythe followed him out of the elevator, trying for a brief, sad smile.

Silence. Neither Candy nor Garth moved.

"What were you doing in the frigging elevator?" Candy asked.

"I went outside to call another councilman who'd offered me some inside information," Max said, "and while I waited to come back up, Blythe appeared."

"The elevator was going down," Garth said.

"Somebody had pushed the button for the top floor before I remembered to push the button for Sacha's floor," Blythe said, feeling she ought to contribute something to this inventive tale.

"Don't leave now," Max said. "Let's all stay and enjoy the party now that Blythe has joined...*Garth*," and as he emphasized the word, he smiled serenely at Candy. "And then the three of you can go home together."

Candy's lower lip pushed out. "I don't want to go home together."

"Unfortunately that's the way it has to be tonight," Max said, with what Blythe thought was an admirable show of regret. "I have a column to write."

"Shoot!" Candy whined, and stamped her foot.

"I have a reputation to build at the *Telegraph*," Max said.

"Oh, go polish your frigging halo," Candy retorted, and sailed back toward Sacha's door.

"Blythe, I'm so glad you could come by after all," Sacha said in a properly funereal tone when they'd all followed Candy into the apartment.

The rest of the guests apparently assumed she had simply been there the entire time. Before a sulky Candy, a subdued Garth, a heated-looking Max and Blythe, who was inwardly glowing, left the party, Blythe managed to murmur to Max, "I owe you one."

"Damn sure do," he growled.

"As soon as Candy's had her chance—"

"To hell with Candy. I need you now."

But the snip of conversation reminded him he also owed somebody, so he sidled over to Sacha. "Thanks," he said.

"Anytime," Sacha whispered back. "But someday will you explain to me what the hell is happening here? Like, is it something I could use in my option book?"

"WHEN'S THE FUNERAL?" Garth said. He and Candy and Blythe sat in a tense little triangle in the living room, Candy stretched out on the sofa and Garth lounging gracefully in the comfortable armchair with his Italian loafers on the ottoman. Blythe fluttered around the apartment. She couldn't sit still. What she wanted to do was go to bed and hold the memories of Max to her heart.

"Ah. The funeral. It's—" *just pick a time* "—it's tomorrow morning."

"I'm sorry about this foster aunt," Candy said, unexpectedly sending a sympathetic expression in Blythe's direction. "I hope you'll tell me about her sometime when things aren't so busy, like which of your foster families she belonged to, and did you feel close to her."

"Yes, yes, I will," Blythe stammered. "As you said, when things aren't so busy."

"But if the funeral's in the morning," Candy said, cheering up, "you can still go with Garth to his conference banquet. It will make you feel better."

"What conference banquet?"

"The one I have to go to tomorrow night. Candy said you could go as my guest." Garth didn't sound particularly enthusiastic.

Blythe uttered an exasperated sigh. "Well, it's news to me."

"I told you about it, didn't I?" Candy said. "Black-tie?"

"I've already signed you up," Garth said to Blythe, although he was gazing at Candy. "You know," he added, leaning back and looking nostalgic, "every time I put on a tux I remember taking Sandi Gilbreth to the senior prom."

"She was certainly...memorable," Candy said, sounding unnecessarily snappish, Blythe thought.

"She was the most beautiful girl," Garth said, "so I—"

"She was *not*," Candy said, sitting upright on the

sofa. "She was *attractive*, sure, but the reason the guys liked her was that she put out."

"Candy!" Garth said. "Hey, you were only in the ninth grade then. What did you know about things like that?"

"When you spend the weekdays with your mother and her current boyfriend, and the weekends with your father and his bimbo," Candy said grimly, "you learn early."

Blythe realized she'd stopped fluttering and was listening. A puzzling dynamic was shaping up between Candy and Garth. He was a little older than she was, so maybe he hadn't noticed that the hot little freshman who lived next door to him was lusting after the handsome senior boy who lived next door to her....

But maybe now he was really looking at her, realizing this tall beauty wasn't the girl next door anymore. And even though Candy was pursuing Max, she didn't seem to like Garth's memories of another woman.

Of course, she was simply shoving Blythe at him. Maybe she was imagining things. It bore thinking about, but right now all she felt was tired. The glow Max had generated in her was dying down from pure exhaustion, and she kept hearing rebellious voices in her head. She wasn't sure she could take many more nights sleeping on the sofa. She didn't like the idea of having to sneak into Candy's bathroom in the morning for her shower, didn't like having to pick out her clothes the night before so she could escape from the apartment before Garth woke up.

In short, she'd had one glorious night with Max, followed by two days in which she'd somehow gotten fed up with her entire life. Tomorrow was Garth's last day in town, and—whee—she got to go to the "prom" with him before he left.

Then surely she could get back control over her own life.

She felt those dangerous prickles in her scalp that meant her temper was rising. An occupational hazard of being a redhead, or so she'd heard from her several foster parents who'd insisted she put a lot of emotional energy into keeping that temper down, getting along, *going* along, thinking of others instead of herself.

She'd done a good job of it. She'd done *too* good a job of it. But something about making love with Max was changing everything inside her. Damned if she'd just sit back and wait quietly until the situation settled down by itself.

Behind her, Candy and Garth were still sniping at each other. Now they'd moved on to Candy's shameless behavior with the quarterback, and as Blythe listened, Candy countered with a vividly nasty description of the first girl Garth had brought home from undergraduate school at Brown. Among the little tart's many faults and failings, she'd referred to her parents as "Mummy and Popsy."

"It's been *great* seeing you again," Candy was wrapping up. "It's made me remember things I'd forgotten about you. Now I think I'll be just as happy to see you leave."

I'd be happy to see you leave right now.

"Well. Guess what," Garth said, sounding like a fifth-grader. "I'm not leaving quite as soon as you think I am. I've canceled my appointments through Wednesday to stay here and do some research at the NYU hospital system. So there."

Blythe was thinking murderous thoughts.

"I'll move to a hotel and get out of your hair," Garth finished up.

Thank the Lord.

"Oh, no, you don't have to do that," Candy said with a deep sigh. "I'll just keep to my room while you're around. Or Max's apartment," she added dreamily.

That did it. No more Ms. Nice Girl! Starting tomorrow, Candy and Garth could be looking for Blythe the Hun to ride over the crest of the hill, on the attack and determined to conquer!

IT MIGHT BE SUNDAY, but due to the blackout, it was just an ordinary day at the *Telegraph*.

"How's it going, kid," Bart said early that morning.

"About how you'd expect," Max said, and dropped into a hard wooden visitor's chair with a thud. "There's a conspiracy afoot in City Council. Everybody says he wants to give me the real scoop but all they really want to do is—"

"Not City Council," Bart said. "The Candy, Blythe, Garth, Macth thituation." He halted, reddening. "I mean—"

"See?" Max shouted. "Blythe and Garth do not belong together. They're nominally incompatible."

"What?"

Max got his frustration under control. "Here's how it's going down, Bart. Since Blythe promised Candy she wouldn't see me again, it somehow means I end up going out with Candy every night and leaving Blythe alone with Garth. Now nobody asked me if I wanted to go out with Candy every night. It just seems to happen that way. It's *understood* in some weird, mystical way by the three of them. I don't understand it at all, but somehow I showed up last night just the way I was supposed to."

He paused. "I'm not that stupid," he muttered. "I showed up hoping I'd see Blythe. Hoping that psycho Brandon would get tied up in a discussion on lithium levels or something, and Candy wouldn't be home yet and—"

"You've fallen for Blythe," Bart said, sounding oddly dreamy and abnormally happy.

"I barely know her," Max snapped. "I just think I'd like to know her. That's all. And I'm positive I don't want to know Candy any better than I already do."

"You may not have a choice." Bart was back to glum again.

"Of course I have a choice." He was feeling the heat of rage in his face and reminded himself again to calm down.

Bart went on as if he hadn't spoken. "Candy has that effect on people," he said. "Like, it's just understood that she'll go out and get the facts—does a damned good job of it, too—and Blythe will rewrite the story so it doesn't sound like it was pecked out at random by monkeys."

Max frowned. "Does she get any credit for it?"

"No. It's Candy's story."

"That's not fair."

"It works."

"It doesn't help Blythe's career."

"I have a paper to get out. I'm not responsible for career-building."

"Yeah, yeah," Max said with a quick smile. "You talk tough, but you feel guilty. I can see it in your eyes." Actually, Bart's eyes reminded him of a basset hound's. A guilty basset hound.

Bart leaned forward, put his hands on his desk and rested his jowls on them, looking exactly like a guilty basset hound as he gazed up at Max. "Okay, okay," he muttered. "I know Blythe hates her job. I know she feels like she's at a dead end. And she feels worse because Candy took off like a skyrocket."

Max squirmed a little in his chair. "Maybe Blythe doesn't even want an all-consuming career the way Candy seems to." He tried to say it casually, as if it didn't really matter.

"Oh, yeah, she does," Bart sighed. "Maybe even more than Candy does."

It had been too much to hope for anyway, that Blythe might like to make a career of homemaking the way his mother had. "Why do you say 'even more than Candy'?"

"Because Blythe doesn't have a fallback position like Candy does, like you do, for that matter. If she runs out of money, she really runs out of money. She's still looking for an identity, too." Bart winced at his own psychobabble. "Something to define her as a person. Most of us get that from our folks, and Blythe didn't have any."

"This means she's scared to start looking for another job, right? So you'll try to give her a boost here at the *Telegraph*?" However dashed his hopes were, if Blythe wanted and needed a successful career, he intended to bust his balls getting it for her.

"Now hold on," Bart protested.

"Just think about it," Max said.

"Moving van come yet?"

"Hell, no," Max said.

"You'll feel better when your stuff comes," Bart said.

"I don't give a damn about my *stuff*," Max said, then

stomped back upstairs to his cubicle. He'd feel better if he could call Blythe, but he didn't want Garth or, worse, Candy to answer.

Tiger Templeton, the van driver, called. Max was starting to worry about his sexual orientation, the way his heart had begun to pound when he heard the guy's voice. "Where are you?" he said, his pulse speeding up.

"We had to spend the night upstate," Tiger said. He sounded pretty morose about it. "We lost a knob."

"Buy a new one and get on the frigging road!" He'd spent way too much time with Candy.

"It's the original knob off an antique dresser. Not available in any store."

"Come on!" Max said. "If it's lost, it's lost. You have insurance to cover it, right?"

Tiger's voice was hushed. "This is a dresser that moved west from Boston over two hundred years ago. It's signed. It's appraised at forty-seven thousand dollars. You want me to get my insurance canceled?"

The sum even shut Max up for a minute.

"We've searched the truck, we've searched your stuff, we may have to go back to Cincy and search Mrs. Edwards's stuff."

"Right! So bring my stuff and then go back to Mrs. Edwards. If I find a knob, I'll turn it in. Scout's honor."

"The dealer doesn't see it that way. He'll turn the loss in to the insurance company if we leave before he has his knob. So I'm thinking late tomorrow. Maybe Tuesday."

"Don't get my hopes up," Max said. "I can only take so much heartbreak."

"Huh?"

"Never mind. I'll see you when I see you."

. With everything else weighing him down, he was going to have to go to a Laundromat. There was a limit to the number of times you could use a towel.

BY SUNDAY MORNING, Blythe was beginning to think, *Who needs children with Candy and Garth around?* Her most uncomfortable moments with Garth, she thought about it, were when Candy was around, so she felt a great sense of relief when her roommate had to leave early Sunday morning to cover a mugging in Central Park, and Garth stopped making the suggestive comments he never made when Blythe was alone with him.

When the door closed behind a subdued and perfectly nice Garth, who'd made her bed and practically sterilized her bathroom after using it, Blythe the Hun got to work on her battle strategy. She'd asked Bart for a half day off to attend the "funeral," and he'd mumbled his permission. She'd use the time to carry out her plan.

It was going to cost a fortune. She would think of it as an investment in her future. First she packed a bag, carefully choosing an outfit that wouldn't wrinkle, and then she addressed the more complicated aspects of the coup she intended to make this very evening.

Early in the afternoon, her mission accomplished, she called Max at his office number. When she got his voice mail, she simply said, "Call me. I have a plan."

When Max returned to his office after yet another attempt to follow the paper trail left by a councilman who was suspected of taking bribes from construction companies, he got the message and dialed her work number. He was thrilled when she answered.

"What?" he practically panted. "What is it?"

"I'll have that ready in about ten minutes," she said

briskly. "I'm working on a story of Candy Jacobsen's right now. You're next on my list."

"Damn," he said, and hung up.

She called him as soon as Candy left her office. "Max," she said breathlessly, "I have to tell you what I've done. I've..."

"Tell you what," Max answered. "I've got somebody here right now. I'll call you back as soon as I'm free."

Candy was a fast walker. She'd left Blythe's cubicle and gone straight upstairs to Max's.

And he still hadn't called her back when she had to go home to get ready for her big night at the shrinks' conference. Maybe he'd come by, call her at home before Garth and Candy got there.

She was about to snap. Tonight mattered to her. A lot.

8

BLYTHE WAS DRESSED WHEN Garth came home. Since Candy had left instructions with the doorman and given him a key, he came through the door unannounced a few minutes after she'd sat down at a little table in the living room to write a note to Max about her daring plan for the evening.

"Great dress," he said, then hesitated. "Does it have a jacket to go with it?"

"Yes," she said, crumpling the note in her palm. "I'll put it on now if it would make you feel more comfortable." He'd surprised her in the red charmeuse strapless number she'd found at a resale shop. It certainly had a jacket, which was long-sleeved, high-necked and as forbidding as the dress was sexy. And it was quite significant that he wanted her to put it on.

Early this morning she'd awakened from a nightmare in which Garth gave up his practice in Boston and moved in with her and Candy. In the dream, he and Candy occupied the two bedrooms while she slept beside the fireplace, clothed in rags.

This apartment didn't have a fireplace. They'd have to change apartments. It would be up to her to organize the move.

She had to remind herself that the Cinderella phase of her life was officially over. "Excuse me," she said primly, and stuck one arm into the jacket. The note went into the jacket, too, bulging out just below her elbow. After stuffing her other arm in, she buttoned the jacket all the way up to her chin before she faced him again.

"That's good," Garth said. "Give me a minute and I'll get into the old penguin suit." He went to her room and closed the door.

In that one moment, Blythe figured out what was going on. His interest in her was all a show for Candy. Emboldened by this sudden realization, Blythe went to the kitchen, pulled the note out of her sleeve, smoothed out the wrinkles as well as she could and resumed writing instructions to Max.

"The speech tonight should be great," Garth called out to her from her room. "Dr. Donald Durwood is speaking on the treatment of trauma-induced adult-onset psychoses. He's tops in the field."

Blythe felt she might be getting a few of those adult-onset psychoses, but she was glad to hear about the speech. "Sounds super," she enthused. "I hope he gets into the topic really thoroughly."

"Oh, he will," Garth said. "I've never heard him speak for less than an hour."

"That would be after the dinner, right?"

"Yes."

"Followed by a question and answer session?"

Garth stuck his head out the door, and Blythe stopped writing. "Do you have a question for Durwood?"

"I might," Blythe said.

Garth looked gratified. "You're really getting into the spirit of the evening," he said.

The sound of the buzzer sent her to the phone on the

kitchen wall. "Mr. Laughton is here for Miss Candy," the night doorman announced.

Blythe tensed. She had one chance to make this work. "Send him up," she said, then started back to the kitchen to get the half-written note.

"Who was that?" Garth asked through the partly open bedroom door.

She halted. "Max. He's here to pick up Candy."

"Wonder where she is."

"Out on a story, I imagine," Blythe said, then heard a couple of sharp raps on the door.

"Can you get it?" Garth said. "I'm putting in a cuff link."

With a longing look at the kitchen where the note lay, Blythe opened the door. Max stood there, big and graceful, casually dressed and sexy as all hell. He gazed at her in her primly buttoned red satin. "Going out?" he said.

"Yes, she is," Garth said, disappointingly materializing behind her. "With me. Hello, Laughton."

"Brandon," Max said. He looked disappointed, too, even though Garth had at last remembered his name.

All three of them, disappointed in one way or the other, and the evening hadn't even started yet. Her plan would lift the disappointment level of at least two of them. Blythe felt a bolt of panic. Garth looked as if he intended to whisk her away, and she had to get that note to Max. "I'm afraid Candy's not home yet," she said.

"Oh, well, then," Max said. "I'll just wait for her in the lobby."

"Absolutely not," Blythe exclaimed. "Come right in. Make yourself a drink." She gave him a meaningful look. It was imperative that he go to the kitchen and see her note. She hadn't finished it, but she'd put down the pertinent information, she thought.

"I'll make him a drink," Garth said, getting a stubborn look on his face.

"I can do it," Max said, staring at Blythe, probably trying to figure out the meaning of her meaningful look. "You both look like you're ready to party."

"We have a few minutes." Garth looked as if he wondered about the meaning of the meaningful look, too. "Still a Scotch addict?" He headed for the kitchen.

Blythe gave Max a push and he followed Garth at a clip. "I'm not addicted to anything, Brandon."

"Everybody likes a change of pace now and then," Blythe said, scurrying after them. The liquor cupboard was just above the spot where she'd left the note. In the kitchen, she dived in front of the two men. "We have bourbon, gin—" she couldn't reach the top shelf even in her high-heeled gold sandals, so she grabbed for a bottle on the lower shelf "—and crème de menthe." She put the bottle down firmly over the note. "That's what you'd like, I bet. A nice crème de menthe."

Max made a face, but he moved up beside her at the counter. "Sounds great."

"You're kidding," Garth said.

"No!" Max said. "What could be better on a warm summer night than something minty?" With his stomach right up to the kitchen counter and the two of them shielding his actions, he grabbed the note. Blythe's heart sank when it didn't move. It was stuck to the bottom of the bottle. They never did anything with crème de menthe but pour it over ice cream. Somebody had dribbled.

She picked up the bottle and ripped off the note,

which Max shoved between two of the buttons of his shirt. "I'll get you a clean cocktail napkin."

"Was that a napkin?" Garth inquired. "Because it looked to me like a..."

"Shopping list," Blythe said. "But it's okay. There wasn't much on it." She opened the cupboard below the sink and pretended to be throwing the note away.

"Cheers," Max said. He swiftly poured himself a short glass of green glop, turned to face Garth, took a sip and smiled.

Garth's expression said there was no accounting for tastes.

Blythe hoped Max's chest wouldn't rustle. Next she wondered how much of the note had been wiped out by the greenish-black ring the bottle had made.

She drifted out of the kitchen, relieved when Max followed. "Garth is taking me to his big conference dinner," she said. "Black-tie. It's at the *Carlyle Hotel*, you know, right around the corner from where they've been having the conference." She emphasized the words. "It's going to be such fun." She began to speak more rapidly. "Dr. Damon Dunwoody's going to talk about grown-ups who go crazy. His speech ought to start at about *eight-thirty*. It will probably make the news—"

Garth burst out of the kitchen as if he'd been shot from a cannon. "It's Donald Durwood," he said in a truly annoyed voice, "and do not, under any circumstances, use the word *crazy* at this event. Durwood's talking about adult-onset—"

Blythe whirled toward Garth. At this point, Candy burst through the apartment door and Max whirled toward her. "Well, here we are, together again," Blythe said, feeling dizzy.

"But not for long," Garth said. "Now we really must go." He shifted his gaze toward Candy. Blythe looked in her direction to find her gazing at Garth, who was admittedly stunning in the most perfectly fitted tuxedo Blythe had ever seen, with the whitest tucked shirt and a bow tie that had been hand-tied. His studs and cuff links looked like real onyx. "Well, aren't we glamorous?" Candy said, tearing herself away from Garth to give Blythe an assessing look. "What are we doing tonight, Max?"

"Chowing down on barbecue at Brother Jimmy's," Max said. "Unless you'd prefer the Hog Pit downtown."

Candy flinched. "Yum," she said. Blythe thought she looked tired for once. Too tired?

Too much to ask for. All Blythe could do was trust Max to figure out her note and act on it.

ONCE HE AND CANDY HAD placed their order at Brother Jimmy's, Max faked a need to powder his nose to get a look at the note tucked inside his shirt. It said, "Dear Max," and below that was a fat, sticky ring of vintage crème de menthe. A few words were still readable, though, and two numbers she'd written at the very end. The first one was obviously a phone number, but the other one... A room number? A hotel room? In the Carlyle Hotel where she was going with Garth?

His heart pounded. She'd gone on and on about that speech, and she'd said it would start at about eight-thirty. She must have meant something by it.

He called the hotel and asked for Blythe Padgett. His heart zinged with anticipation when the operator connected him, but when he reached voice mail, he hesitated. What if she had gotten the room for Garth and just wanted him to know the creep was no longer making himself at home in her bedroom?

He chewed his lower lip for a second, deciding that he'd still have to find out. Then, of course, he had one more call to make.

"Not again," Bart groaned.

"A quick call at eight-fifteen," Max cajoled him.

"Is your father about to have another heart attack?"

"No, I've been too hard on Dad. This time it'll be a call from a Deep Throat councilman."

Thoughtfully, he wended his way back to the table and sat down amongst the chewed ribs and barbecue sauce spills. "Just think," he said. "This was only the starter course. Where's the beef?"

Candy was arresting, or arrestable, in a dress that measured exactly the distance from the tops of her breasts to a spot one inch below where her underpants would end, if she was even wearing any. The dress should have turned him on. Instead his mind was totally focused on Blythe in red satin from neck to arch. So while Candy poured herself fluidly over him, he counted down the seconds to eight-fifteen when Bart had promised to call.

"YES, I THINK BEING orphaned affected me in a number of ways. For one thing, I had no parents." The other seven people at the table—psychiatrists, psychologists or spouses, who probably had to listen to psyche analysis every night at dinner—were intensely fascinated by her orphaned state and gazing at her raptly. She was touched by their interest and wished she could say something fascinating to them, but her mind was on the daring caper she was about to pull off. "I didn't have a mother to borrow clothes from," she rambled

on. "My foster mothers had clothes, of course, but...
Oh, look, dessert, and doesn't it look wonderful."

"When does the speech start?" she hissed at Garth,
attacking a tall pile of meringue squares, pie crust
squares and creamy fillings.

He smiled at her. "I don't think I've ever seen a lay-
person so excited about sitting through a highly technical speech."

"Highly technical, huh?" Blythe had had a couple of
glasses of wine to bolster her courage for the thing she
was about to do—had already half done, considering
the time, money and deviousness she'd put into it. But,
if anything, the wine seemed to be making her more
nervous.

When this phase of her life was over, she planned to
spend the rest of it doing good unto others. Volunteer
work. Maybe the Peace Corps in some anaconda-
infested jungle. It was going to take something big to
make up for the way she was behaving right now.

And so deliberately. Misbehavior in cold blood.

"Uh-huh," she murmured to Garth to make him
think she'd been listening to the explanation of Durwood's work he'd launched into. She dropped her
gaze to her watch. It was eight twenty-one. Her heart
dropped to the pit of her stomach. She'd gone to all this
trouble, and the banquet chairman wasn't cooperating
with her schedule.

"You really can't wait." Garth sounded amused and
approving.

"Well, if it's too technical..." she hedged. "Hurry up.
Eat your dessert."

Waiters flowed among the lavender-draped tables in
the Carlyle Ballroom with silver carafes of coffee. Coffee had to mean the end was near.

"Why hurry?" Garth said. "We can eat during the speech."

Blythe wanted to strangle him, but she couldn't, of course, because that would tip him off to her secret agenda. Every time she thought about it she got twitchy, wriggly, just imagining the delights she could pack into a one-hour speech.

With enormous relief, she saw a waiter approaching their table with coffee. It wouldn't be long now. She counted the cups as the waiter poured, one cup, two cups, three, four, and then a woman across the table said, "Is it decaf?"

"No, madam, but I'll bring decaffeinated."

"Oh, it's not decaf?" The chorus went all the way around the table. Blythe was deeply frustrated to see all the filled cups going back on the tray, to see the waiter vanish, to know that time was flying.

"I guess they thought we needed caffeine to get through Don's speech," said the psychiatrist to Blythe's right. His expression spoke volumes of professional jealousy.

"I did," Blythe said glumly. The little poke in the knee Garth gave her irritated the daylights out of her. So much for him. It made her feel a little less bad about saying, "From what Garth tells me, I'd better make a trip to the powder room beforehand, if you'll excuse me please."

She rose in a flurry, seeing an anxious look cross Garth's face when a voice boomed a welcome from the podium. "Continue to enjoy this excellent dessert and coffee while the program begins. Our speaker for the evening needs no introduction, but..."

Just in case, I'm going to give him a really long one.

At least that's what Blythe hoped the man had in

mind as she ignored Garth's, "Blythe, you're going to miss the beginning of the speech," and flew from the room.

She went straight for the elevator, whipping out the plastic key to the room she'd checked into as soon as the hotel would allow it. She raced down the hall to the room, and tugging off her jacket, dived into her suitcase for the one essential item the evening required. Well, one of the two essential items. And in case Max wasn't prepared, she'd brought both items.

If he didn't show up, she'd have to take a cold shower before she rejoined Garth.

MAX RESTED HIS WRIST ON ONE thigh and took a peek at his watch. It was 8:22 p.m. and Bart hadn't called. He felt like quitting and going back to Chicago. He was sure that Candy's last nibbly kiss to his neck had left a hickey he'd have to explain to Blythe. From now until this charade ended, he was checking out restaurants and making sure they didn't have booths. He needed a nice hard table between himself and Candy. He'd eaten so many ribs and so much barbecued beef just trying to postpone the moment she'd invite herself home with him that he wasn't sure he could even stand up, and now he was urging dessert on her.

"I'll have the peach cobbler," she purred, "and let me tell you how I'd like it served. *Where* I'd like it served."

If the opposite of an erection was a contraction, that's what he was having. "Candy, be nice," he said, trying to sound like Garth, the last person in the world he'd ever want to sound like.

"You wouldn't believe how nice I am," she said. "I'm going to be the nicest—"

His cell phone rang. He was limp with relief as he shouted, "Hello" into it, realizing he hadn't made any attempt to hide it and stopping himself just before adding, "Where in the hell have you been?"

"Sorry," Bart's sorry voice answered. "Linda's mother called. The woman has timing. I could tell you stories—"

"Well, couldn't you—" He calmed himself down before he blew it by reminding Bart he had a cell phone like the rest of the twenty-first-century folks. Or maybe Bart didn't. Blythe didn't. "Couldn't you make it another night? I'm pretty busy here."

"I bet you are. Honest to God, Max, you're more trouble now than you were when you were two. So go on. Entertain me. Linda's bitching at me for being curt, that's what she said, curt, with her sainted mother—"

"Has to be tonight." Max frowned at the phone.

"I'm going with you," Candy said.

"Hold on a second, Councilman," Max said. "What did you say?" he asked Candy.

"I said I'm going with you to this emergency meeting with whichever councilman you're talking to."

The look on Candy's face was so stubborn she reminded Max of a bulldog. "You can't," he whispered. "This is the inside scoop, the info I've been hoping for—"

"I'm going with you."

"It's out of the question." Max did his own bulldog face.

"Try to stop me."

Max glared at her. Candy glared back. Max spoke into the cell phone. "The lady wants to come along. Do you mind? I'm sure she's quite discreet."

"I guess the answer to that one would be no?" Bart said.

"Well, yes, she is a journalist, but..."

"So the answer's hell, no."

Max repeated this to Candy verbatim. "I'm not a political reporter," she reminded him. "I'm a crime reporter."

Max repeated this to Bart verbatim. "Just say no," Bart said. "Hurry up. Linda wants to bitch at me some more."

Max did not repeat this. "He says absolutely not. He doesn't trust journalists." Now Max put on his earnest, pleading look. "This could be my big chance," he said, meaning every word of it. "You'd do anything to get a story, wouldn't you? You'd ditch me right here to go after a scoop that would make you famous in newspaper circles and win you a prize?"

Her eyes flickered.

Encouraged, he went on. "You wouldn't deprive me of *my* big chance, would you, Candy?"

"Oh, hell, no," Candy muttered. "Okay, I won't horn in on your frigging meeting." She faced him squarely. "But I'm still going with you to wherever it is you're meeting him. You can stash me somewhere and I'll wait for you."

Max wouldn't have cared to repeat verbatim the words that ran through his head when she said that. They might have taught her a thing or two about swearing, but he didn't have time to argue. He didn't even have time to drop her at the Mark, for example, and then go to the Carlyle himself. Instead, spurred on to recklessness by the possibility of an encounter with Blythe, he whisked Candy to the Carlyle and sat her down in the lobby.

"The Carlyle," she commented on the way in, sounding surprised. "Garth and Blythe are here."

"Maybe you'll see them on their way out," Max said, and raced for the bank of house phones.

Blythe answered, sounding breathless. "I'm on my way up," he told her, breathless himself with relief at hearing her voice.

"Hurry," she said.

That was the one thing she didn't have to remind him to do. All at once he was there, facing a door that had been left ajar. Cautiously he pushed it open, and there was Blythe in the center of a king-size bed wearing strapless red satin with a mask over her eyes, not a costume-party mask, a sleeping mask.

Kinky, sure. But Blythe wasn't kinky. "What's the mask for?"

"I can't see you," she said. Her voice was so faint he could barely hear her. "That's what I promised, that I wouldn't see you."

"Whatever works for you," he muttered hoarsely. He was so overcome by the sight of her, her creamy, faintly freckled shoulders, the elegant upsweep she'd somehow gotten her hair into, with little bits and pieces curling down around her face, that all he wanted to do was sprint to that bed and dive in. But besides the mask, there was another jarring component in this otherwise idyllic scene. The television set was on, and on the screen was a dork talking gibberish.

"I'll just turn this off," he said midsprint.

"No, no," she protested. "I have to watch it. I mean, listen to it."

Max slowed. "Why?"

"Because I have to get back in time to ask Dr. Durwood an intelligent question. Garth thinks I'm in the powder room."

"I know an intelligent question you can ask." He crept forward now, aroused, knowing what he longed for was about to happen, and observed that her mask said, "American Airlines." He smiled.

"What?"

"What will you give me if I tell you," he said, and brushed his mouth across her cheek.

Her hands fluttered up to his shoulders. She brushed them down his arms, ran her fingertips over his face as if she were blind, then sank back on the pillows. "Everything," she said, holding her arms out to him. "Everything we have time for."

9

"I CAN HARDLY BELIEVE I'M HERE, you're here, we're together," Max said, stroking the curls back from her forehead and letting her tug him to her for a kiss. He took her lips lightly, still afraid it might be a dream and that, when he touched her, she'd vanish away.

A soft sound came from her throat, and her caress was as tentative as his. He moved his mouth over hers, taking her with more assurance, wanting her badly but also wanting each moment to last. He felt the tip of her tongue at the corner of his mouth and closed his eyes, sliding his arms around her, pulling her tighter.

But she'd done something very brave and inventive, and he also felt a need to protect her. "We need to get you out of this dress." His voice sounded like that of a man with a bad cold, but it was true that he was having trouble with his respiratory system, could hardly breathe. "Don't want to wrinkle it."

"You can crumple it all you like. I don't care," she said, clinging to him.

But she would later, because she would return to Garth, keep this moment, this hour, he hoped, a secret. He lifted himself away from her, turned her to one side and unzipped the dress slowly, kissing the perfect skin of her back, moving his lips down and down as the zipper opened to reveal more and more of her. His mouth was below her waist now, and he tugged at the silk of her panties, the only thing she wore beneath the dress, to kiss each round, soft cheek of her buttocks. She moaned, almost a protest, but she wriggled, too, and heat shot through his body from his demanding erection.

Slowly he slid the dress off and gazed at her lying there, a small, exquisite woman with those faint freckles covering her whole body. It might take him a lifetime, but he wanted to kiss every freckle.

He got up, laid the dress carefully on a chair and ripped off his own clothes, tossing them on the floor before he lay back down beside her. She'd wiggled beneath the sheets, and he joined her there. Her skin was hot when he pulled her tight against himself, tucking her head under his chin, molding her breasts to his chest, arching her back, pressing his aching erection to the softness of her stomach.

The mask was turning him on, speeding up his pulse rate, urging him to explore her secrets. He ducked his head to her breasts, and being surrounded by those soft, warm mounds was almost more than he could handle. He took a perfect pink nipple into his mouth, rolling his tongue around it, relishing her cry of delight and simply the feel of it, the taste of it. She pressed herself against his insistent arousal, generating an exquisite agony that had him reeling with need.

She sat up so suddenly he almost yelled, "Whiplash!"

"What'd he just say?" she said, sounding anxious.

He frowned at her navel. "The guy making the speech?"

"Yes. Something about eccentricity versus..."

"I have enough competition already," he growled, pulling her back down. "I refuse to compete with *him*."

Her answer was a low, relaxed laugh as she rolled herself sinuously over him, covering him like a pool of warm maple syrup. Her nipples hardened against his chest and he felt the wetness of her as she opened up to him, framing him in velvet, then clenching those muscles until he was cocooned in nearly unbearable pleasure. He was floating, sinking, drowning in her sweetness. "Nobody can compete with you," she said, sliding up his heaving body until he felt the wetness at his waist, moving up his chest.

He slid down, tugging on silken cheeks to speed up her journey, until at last, she settled over his waiting mouth, his searching tongue, and he felt her clutch the headboard as she cried out, arched her back, moved against him while he devoured her hungrily.

She moved against him, faster and faster. The bed rocked with their passion. "Oh, please," she moaned, "please, now..." She slid fluidly down him. "Now, now... Running...out of time..."

"I don't have condoms," he gasped. "Too dangerous...with Candy around..."

"I know." She was breathless, too, and her breasts slid across his face as she reached over him. He captured one taut tip with his mouth, but only for a second. "I have some."

He felt her press the packet into his hand. "I want to put it on you, slowly..."

His blood reached the boiling point.

"...but I can't see you. You'll have to do it." He speedily followed her order and let her tug him inside her, where he wanted to be, where she clearly wanted him, both of them consumed by the thrusting, the pulling back, the thrusting again, battling with each other and both winning.

He felt the flood build up in her body, felt it in the way she writhed against him, her head flung back, her fingers gripping his shoulders in the mindless animal motion of pure passion, and heard it in the thin little cry that escalated into a shriek of pure pleasure. He came into her, hard, almost painfully at first, then feeling the waves of relief as she collapsed against him, still moving, still shaking with spasms.

BLYTHE WAS FRIGHTENED by the intensity of her feelings. Her night with Max hadn't been a magical, one-time-only coming together of unusual events. It was real. All nights with Max would be like this. She wanted to spend all her nights with Max. She couldn't resign herself to stolen moments, never knowing when the next one might become possible, convenient. It was madness to sacrifice this pure pleasure on the altar of good manners. As she clung to him, her mind drifted off into thrilling dreams of future nights while her body zinged with afterglow and hints of reawakening desire, a lust for more. Now.

She came to her senses when applause emerged from the television set. With a shriek, she leaped directly off him and landed with her feet on the floor. "I have to go," she said, her voice shaking.

"You're going to give me a heart attack one of these days." His voice was a husky groan.

"I'm sorry, but I have to get back down there and ask a question."

"You can't. You can't leave now."

"I have to! I...I just have to." She fumbled for her panties, scooted her feet around the floor in search of her shoes.

Max knew she had to go back to Garth. This moment

had been a treasured gift she'd struggled hard to give him. He decided he'd better help her out, and slipped a shoe on each foot, then dropped the red dress over her head.

"Dr. Durwood has generously offered to field questions from the audience," the master of ceremonies droned from the screen. "Yes, the gentleman on the left..."

Max had a burning question of his own. "Any possibility you can get back here tonight?" He zipped up her dress and handed her the jacket.

"I intend to try."

"Me, too." Candy's bulldog expression crossed his mind.

"I put the other key on the dresser."

Max grabbed for it, held it while he stepped into his trousers, then put it in his pocket. "No hard feelings if the other one doesn't show up."

"Right. We're just trying to keep our promises, keep the peace, avoid hurt feelings. We shouldn't go downstairs together," Blythe said, "just in case."

Forget "just in case." "Absolutely not. I'll go first," Max puffed, hopping on one foot and then the other to get back into his socks and shoes.

"But Durwood's already answered one question. I've got to get in there with mine. What am I going to ask him?" she worried. "It's got to be good, and I just—"

"I have to go down first because Candy's waiting in the lobby."

The mask still hid her eyes, but Blythe's mouth was a startled oval. "Candy's been waiting in the lobby while we—"

"She insisted on coming. By the way, you're still a councilman, in case anybody asks."

"Wow. Public office, and so young. Okay. Go! Really fast." She was tugging on her jacket and stabbing the buttons into their holes.

He grabbed her and gave her a hard, desperate kiss. "You are one fabulous lady," he whispered, and left, running down the hall and willing his shaking legs to keep working.

He reached the lobby and grabbed Candy out of her chair so abruptly that she squealed and tossed the newsmagazine she'd been reading into the lap of a startled man in the same seating area. "Max, what's with you?" she asked as he hurried her out of the Carlyle.

"Got a column to write," he said breathlessly.

Out of the corner of his eye he saw a flash of red scurrying toward the stairs to the Grand Ballroom. Could she get back to that room upstairs later? Could he get back to that flash of red? He intended to give it a damned good try.

"Well, I must say you took your frigging time," Candy was saying. "That frigging councilman had better have delivered some frigging juicy stuff. And speaking of juicy..."

Max groaned. The word *juicy* set off all sorts of sensations. Off to the races. Race. The race to get back to that room and Blythe.

BLYTHE FLEW INTO THE Grand Ballroom, still buttoning her jacket, and collapsed into the first empty chair she ran across, relieved to hear Durwood going on and on in his answer to the last question, which must have been awfully dull, because Durwood's answer was just as dull.

The other thing she saw was Garth's head swiveling, looking for her. She tried to send a reassuring wave, but as short as she was, he didn't seem to see her. So there was no reason, except that it was a great big lie, that she couldn't tell him she'd been waving all through the speech, but as short as she was, she couldn't possibly have gotten his attention without distracting the audience.

As Durwood wound down, she raised her hand. The perfect question had come to her on the elevator, when she was still zinging from being with Max and thinking she might want to zing with Max for the rest of her life. She didn't merely raise her hand, she waved it and, for good measure, jumped up and down a few times.

"Yes," the emcee said, "the little lady in the back, in the red dress."

A moderator rushed toward her with a microphone. She took it, straightened her spine, thought of herself as Blythe the Hun and spoke into it. "Dr. Durwood, do you recognize the currently popular term *sexual addiction*, and do you include it in your list of adult-onset psychoses?"

Because if he did, she had it. But she didn't think she was addicted to sex. She was addicted to Max. And while she was still recreating the lovely, stolen interlude with him in her mind, Garth's head swiveled again. This time, he spotted her.

"I know the term," Durwood said, "and it certainly is adult-onset, but I'm not sure I'd call it a psychosis." And then he smiled.

"I think," he went on, speaking over the low rumble

of laughter that came from the audience, "that 'sexual addiction' is one of those phrases that has become…"

Blythe tuned him out. She'd done her job and could take a minute to daydream—or fifteen minutes, given the way Durwood enjoyed hearing himself speak.

"Where were you?" The minute the Q and A session had ended, Garth had honed in on her at her spot in the back.

"I didn't want to take attention away from the speech by walking all the way down there when there was a perfectly good seat at the back of the room."

He gazed at her. "You must have heard the speech," he said thoughtfully, as if he'd been doubting it, "to have asked such a provocative question."

Wow. Her question had been *provocative*. "I only missed a little bit of the beginning," Blythe assured him.

"Impressive, wasn't it? He's a man ahead of his time."

Or he might be behind the times. How would she know? "I heard the speech. Didn't say I understood it," she said.

"I didn't even understand *all* of it," Garth said with a slight smile.

Something new was in his voice, something more subdued in his attitude. She felt something new for him, too. Sympathy. The conversation between him and Candy the night before came back to her, drumming in her ears, and she suddenly knew she had the key to solving the problem that was making all four of them unhappy. "Could we talk for a few minutes?" Blythe said.

"Sure. Let's go to the bar. Have a nightcap."

They sat at a small table in a corner and both ordered

Perrier. It felt wonderful fizzing down Blythe's throat, while desire for Max still sizzled through her body and hope bubbled up in her heart.

"Blythe."

"What?" Had her attention been wandering?

"When you asked Durwood that question, were you thinking about Candy?"

Candy had been the last thing on her mind. It was only a question, and an inspired one at that. "No," she said.

"You don't think Candy might be addicted to sex?"

Asking the question, he didn't sound clinical. He sounded like a man who wanted to know the worst— and the best—about a woman he cared for. "No, I don't," she said gently. "I think early on Candy decided to use a sexy attitude to get male attention, like some other girl might use her sense of humor or her ability to sing at parties."

"She needs masculine attention," Garth said worriedly.

"We all do," Blythe said.

"But not the amount of masculine attention Candy needs. Constant masculine attention from many males, every male..."

While Blythe wanted masculine attention from just one man, a man she could attract with good cooking, a pretty house and a maternal instinct, this was Garth's therapy session, not hers. "Candy may need it more than some women. I don't think she ever spent a minute alone with her dad. He always had some beautiful younger woman around."

Garth gave her a slight smile. "You should join the profession."

Blythe waved off the compliment. "That's just good common sense," she said. "Candy's an open book."

"She is *not*." Garth's eyes widened.

Now Blythe was truly seeing light at the end of the tunnel. "Let's talk about us for a minute," she said.

Garth looked as if he were having to shift gears, but eventually he said, "There isn't an 'us,' is there, Blythe?"

"No," she said, and patted his hand.

"Candy knew what she was doing when she invited me down here, though," Garth said. "You and I are a lot alike."

"Yes," Blythe said, "and that makes me wonder... You don't seem like a person who would agree to go to bed with a stranger. Why did you tell Candy you would?"

To her surprise, he blushed and shifted his gaze away. "Here's how dumb I am," he said with a self-deprecating little laugh. "I thought...well, I thought Candy was talking about herself when she said, 'I have a friend with a problem.' I've known Candy since she was about four, and I've wanted to make love with her since she was about eighteen, and I thought she'd finally—"

"Oh, Garth," Blythe said. "I should have guessed sooner."

"You guessed?"

She smiled at him. "Every pass you made at me was to make Candy jealous, wasn't it? Because you only acted that way when she was around."

Garth drew his eyebrows together. "Maybe it was to make her jealous. Maybe it was because that's what she'd told me to do. Maybe I was trying to distract you from Max because Candy wanted him. You know,

Blythe, we've got to stop letting the woman boss us around."

Blythe laughed. "That's for sure." Then her smile faded. "I feel better knowing somebody who sees her faults as clearly as I do and still loves her just as I do. You can understand, can't you, how kind she's been to me?"

"Oh, yes," Garth said. "See, I was the neighborhood nerd, and it was that feisty, naughty little blond Jacobsen girl who made the rest of the kids include me in all the mischief they got into."

"No kidding."

"Yeah. I moved in next door, she took one look at me and what she saw was a stray cat that needed to be rescued. And we're talking about a four-year-old brat."

"She never changed," Blythe said. "She did the same thing for me." Her eyes widened. "It just occurred to me, Garth. Max was the new kid on the block. Candy's next stray cat."

A look of pure shock crossed his face. "It's crazy, isn't it," he muttered at last, "that I can figure out these things for other people, but when it comes to me, I'm clueless."

"A common problem," she reassured him. "I'm so glad we talked. I knew that first morning we could be really good friends."

He smiled at her. "Friends forever. Then, as a friend, may I tell you your jacket's buttoned wrong?"

Heat flushed her face as she glanced down at the jacket. She'd skipped a button, and the empty buttonhole pooched out from her rib cage. The jig was up. Garth knew. He didn't know what he knew, he just *knew*.

Slowly she undid the bottom three buttons and redid them correctly. "Thanks, Garth."

"Thank you, Blythe," he said.

"Would you consider the possibility," she said thoughtfully, "that Candy actually invited you here for herself instead of for me? And that she's pursuing Max to show you she's a desirable woman and not a four-year-old brat anymore?"

"No!" Garth exclaimed, but she could tell that, in fact, he was indeed considering it.

While he was paying the waitress, he said, "I can get a hotel room now and I will. I felt bad about you sleeping on the sofa, but..."

"You wanted to be close to Candy." Blythe nodded her understanding. "Don't get a room for tonight. I have one." She fought down another serious blush. "Go back to the apartment. With any luck, Candy will come home and maybe the two of you can talk."

Max didn't come back to the room where she waited for him, hot and hopeful. Blythe refused to consider the possibility that Candy had finally snagged him and, at last, went to sleep. It was the best night's sleep she'd had in days.

10

Max sat on the sofa working on his laptop while Candy dozed on his bed. She'd flatly refused to go home. She would wait while he wrote his article. She'd watch a cable movie while he worked. Then they'd party.

Max wrote a column based on the bits and pieces he'd gleaned from several disgruntled councilmen in phone calls. It wasn't a thrilling exposé, but it raised some interesting questions. He thought it would fly.

Then he wrote an editorial under an assumed name rebutting his own column. That entertained him so much that he went on to write a fake Letter to the Editor declaring the new political columnist to be an arrogant fool.

Then he wrote a short story about a man and a woman who wanted to be together, but couldn't for an absurd, contrived reason.

It was four o'clock in the morning and he was exhausted. The very fact that a World War II documentary was playing in the bedroom indicated that Candy must be asleep, so he laid his head down on the arm of the sofa and closed his eyes.

"I'm going home."

His head shot up from the sofa arm. Candy stood over him, awake and reading his short story straight from the laptop screen.

"It's still rough," he said in a sleep-fogged croak.

"It's a stupid story's what it is."

She gazed at him. For the first time, the predatory look was missing from her face. She was just a beautiful woman looking at him, and looking really mad. "Sorry," he muttered, his head still full of sleep. "I haven't shown you a very good time. I'll take you home. It's late. Or early. It's dark is what I mean."

"That's because you've got your blinds closed. It's almost eight," Candy said. "Besides, anybody who tried to mess with me in the mood I'm in would be mighty frigging sorry." She started for the door, then turned back. "About your story. I get the point." She shook her head. "I never thought I'd see the day when Blythe was getting it from both men and I wasn't getting any."

Max stared at the door, his mouth hanging open for a couple of minutes after she left. Should he chase after her, yelling, "It's just a story"? Should he assure her Blythe wasn't making love with Garth? Should he do something, anything, to soothe her hurt feelings?

No, the truth was he'd undoubtedly hurt her feelings already, over and over. The way he always did, by not being honest with her in the first place. He should have said, "Whatever agreement you and Blythe made is between you two. I'll do what I damned well want to."

He suddenly leaped into action. What he wanted to do was catch Blythe at the hotel, go back there and jump into bed with her. Screw ambition. He was a man consumed with lust.

He dialed the hotel on his cell phone and asked for the room number. She'd already checked out. He muttered softly to himself for a while and then dialed her extension at the *Telegraph*. Unbelievably, she was there.

"Are you alone?" he said, hardly able to believe they might actually have a conversation.

"Yes, and I should be enjoying it, but it's making me nervous. I feel like I'm about to be ambushed."

Max smiled. "I'm sorry I couldn't come back to the hotel last night. I couldn't shake Candy."

Blythe was silent. Too silent. "I wrote until she fell asleep," he said in a hurry, "and she went away mad."

"*I'm* not mad," Blythe said softly. "Just frustrated and feeling guilty."

"You have nothing to feel guilty about."

"But I do." She was warming to his least favorite topic.

"Could we get together and talk about it?"

"Not without making me feel guiltier."

"Just talk. I promise."

"Like I promised Candy I wouldn't see you."

"Kind of like that," he admitted.

"Couldn't we just talk right now?"

"I'd rather hold your hand while we talk."

"Pretend you're holding my hand."

"May I take the phone out on the street and get some coffee while we start talking?"

"Sure."

He must look like a bum, unshaven in wrinkled clothes, but who cared? He started for the elevator.

She was just getting good and wound up about all the kind things Candy had done for her when he reached the first Starbucks, and her list was pretty impressive. Try as he might, Max couldn't get the Candy he knew together in his head with the Candy who'd befriended Blythe, who'd given her a family and friends, who'd made her holidays into normal occasions, well, not normal, but at least occasions that weren't lonely.

"Hold on a second," he said, when the guy next to him in the coffee line spoke to him. "Excuse me?"

"I said are you actually talking to somebody or just holding the phone for effect?"

"I'm listening," Max said.

"Must be a woman," the guy said.

"Yep," Max said. "As you were saying," he said to Blythe, and she was off and running again.

But he'd gotten the picture. She'd already lost too much family. She couldn't afford to lose any more, because Candy was all the family she had left.

He was back in his apartment carrying a café grande with an extra jolt of expresso when she suddenly switched gears. "So we have to make Candy want to release me from my promise."

"Want me to dye my hair orange and start coming to the office in crack-showing jeans?"

"You'd be even more irresistible in orange hair and—what did you call them? Crack-showing jeans? Ugh," Blythe said. "No, we have to get Candy and Garth together. He and I had a talk last night..."

When she finished telling him about her conversation with Garth, Max was stunned. He remembered what Candy had said this morning about Blythe "getting it" from both men. He remembered how subdued Garth had been the last time they were alone and forced to bond, the way Candy had gazed at Garth all dressed up in his tux. "You're a genius," he said, his voice hushed with awe.

"I'll talk to Candy and drop a hint about Garth being

interested in her, not me. Think you can bring yourself to talk to Garth?''

"Sure. I'll come over tonight." He was getting all excited about it. "Think you could arm-wrestle Candy into going out with you for a drink while I tackle Garth at the apartment?''

"Yes," she said in a totally new voice. "I can do the research for you as soon as I finish these galley proofs. Yes. You can count on me."

He took that as a yes for him, too. Blythe had clearly been ambushed by Candy, just as she'd predicted.

BLYTHE PUT DOWN THE PHONE and regarded Candy. She looked different, although Blythe couldn't figure out what the difference was.

"Need some help with a story?" she asked.

"No," Candy said, and slumped into the small, armless chair Blythe had stuffed into her cubicle for visitors, and occasionally to use as a ladder. "I need information."

"Okay," Blythe said, feeling wary.

"I just made a total fool of myself," Candy burst out. "I went home and you weren't there and I couldn't see any evidence you'd slept on the sofa and Garth's door was closed and I just couldn't stand not knowing whether you were in there with him or not so I practically broke down the door and there he was, all by himself, buck naked and getting out of the shower." She sank her head onto Blythe's desk.

"How embarrassing," Blythe murmured.

Candy's head shot up again. "So what I have to know is, are you two frigging sleeping together or not?"

"Not," she said.

"Oh," Candy said, and the wind went right out of her sails.

"To be absolutely truthful with you," Blythe said, intending quite the opposite, "Garth doesn't want to sleep with me."

"Bull."

"No, it's true. Haven't you ever wondered if Garth might have the teeniest little crush on you? Don't you think that's really why he's staying with us instead of at the conference hotel? To get glimpses of you before you go out with Max?"

Candy's mouth hung open. Blythe had never seen her look so uncertain. "Don't be silly," she said at last. "I mean, he's known me all these years without ever giving me a tumble, so how could I possibly think that?"

"Maybe he's always been afraid he's not man enough for you, or afraid you wouldn't be faithful to him, or just plain afraid of you," Blythe persisted. Now that she was already into her talk with Candy, she'd begun to wonder what excuse she could think of for getting her out of the apartment this evening.

"Afraid of me? I'm a pussycat!"

"I'm sorry to tell you, Candy, but you're more like a lioness." *With rabies.*

"Yeah." Candy slumped again, admitting she might appear dangerous to some men. "But Garth's no lap-dog!"

"I'm sure he isn't," Blythe muttered, looking down at her desk.

"You don't know him," Candy said, standing up to glare down at Blythe. "He's the strongest, bravest, most principled man I've ever known, he's steady. The woman who gets Garth will get him for life—"

Blythe felt a sudden jolt of sympathy. Candy's broken home, her parents' several marriages, had taken their toll after all.

"—a hero, a saint, and the most—"

"Sensitive," Blythe chorused with her.

"—man I've ever known! Don't you dare run him down!"

Blythe gazed at her. Candy saw the meaning in her expression. "Okay, I admit it," Candy said finally, back in the chair again and slumping. "I've had the hots for him since I was about...six. Oh, Blythe," she said, "maybe that's why I'm such a slutty bitch. I've been disappointed in love. I've been looking for somebody to fill Garth's place, and there isn't a man in the world strong enough, or—"

"—sensitive enough—" Blythe supplied.

"—to fill his shoes."

"So how are you going to let him know how you feel?" Blythe said, feeling a bit like a psychiatrist herself.

Candy got up, wearing a look of determination. "I'm going back home to jump him."

"Wait a minute, wait a minute..." Blythe was on her feet, chasing Candy down the aisle of the newsroom. Candy moved so fast that Blythe was breathless by the time she caught up with her. "Might I suggest something more subtle?"

"Like you were subtle with Max?" Candy said, but a ghost of a smile hovered on her lips.

"What I did was your unsubtle idea, if you recall," Blythe said primly. "Look, Candy, can we be friends again? Real friends?"

Candy flung both arms around her. By this time they had the attention of the entire newsroom. "Oh, yes," she cried. "I want that more than anything in the world."

"Then let's go out for a drink together after work and discuss a strategy and, well, just talk." In Candy's death grip, Blythe mumbled the words.

"Absolutely. My treat," Candy said. "Okay, I won't jump Garth until I've given subtlety a try."

"Jacobsen, where the hell are you?" The roar came from Bart's office. "We got a murder out in Ozone Park!"

"Guess I'd better take out my energy on getting the frigging story." This time her quick smile was wide and genuine as she strode off. Today she was wearing red and white—a candy cane in motion.

MAX WAS STILL AT HOME GETTING the bad news from Smooth Moves' own Tiger Templeton, who claimed he'd been trying to reach Max for an hour, which Max realized was entirely possible. "Mrs. Edwards saw the knob lying on the floor of the van and put it in her pocket thinking it belonged to a dresser of hers," Tiger reported. "We asked her to FedEx it to us. I'm not sure she understands what FedEx is, but she said her son would come over and help her and how soon could I get her the check to cover the postage. I told her I'd FedEx the check if she'd FedEx the knob, so we've got a thirty-dollar knob here already. Plus phone calls. A lot of them. Long ones. But with any luck, I'll make it to New York tomorrow."

Max couldn't help himself. "There's a two- or three-day FedEx that's cheaper than overnight," he said. "You think her son can talk her out of saving the money?"

"Damn," Tiger said. "Never thought of that. I'll have to call her back."

And at last Max hit the shower. His single bath towel had developed a faintly moldy odor, so he finished up by dotting himself with aftershave. He'd stopped even thinking about using the washcloth and hand towel, and had brought home paper towels. He'd take his clothes to the cleaners this morning, but he suspected he'd have to buy something to wear tomorrow. All in all, it was not a tenable situation.

An hour and a half of traveling up and down to the basement laundry room would have changed his life, but so far he hadn't found that much spare time, what with Candy hanging around. He had a ton of investigating and research to do to stay abreast of the political situation, get out a column a day with a neat balance among local, state, national and international issues, and he wasn't sure how he was going to get it done when he had so many other things on his mind. Mainly sleeping with Blythe. But mixed in with those frustrating images, he was imagining the journey of that knob, inventing an image of old Mrs. Edwards querulously demanding a senior's discount from FedEx for sending the knob, which she would have wrapped in the tiniest box she could find in her cluttered old house, and was going on to berate the FedEx agent for insisting the box had to go in a huge envelope. "Why, my goodness, no wonder FedEx costs so much," Mrs. Edwards would be exclaiming. All these details were playing out in a head that should have been thinking about wrapping up the City Council matter.

He was also playing out the conversation he'd have with Garth this evening. How would he get it started? "Garth, old man, let's have a heart to heart talk." *Max grips Garth's shoulder in a manly, sincere gesture.* No, too phony. "Garth, let's be friends." Bleahh. "Garth, will you get Candy off my back, please?"

The day passed somehow. When he got to the women's apartment, he found Garth staring numbly at a pile of bags and boxes. "What's all that stuff?" he said.

"Cat food. A litter box. Litter. A little bed with a little pillow in it. A scratching post. Toys."

Max looked around. "Everything but the cat," he observed.

"I have a feeling that's a condition that's about to change," Garth said. Now he sounded more dreamy than numb.

Max knelt down beside him. "Garth, there's something I've got to tell you," he said, trying to get the man's attention off the bag of cat litter. "Candy's putting on a good show, but she won't sleep with me. You're a shrink. Maybe you can tell me why. Do you think it might be because you're the one she really wants to be with?"

Which turned out to be exactly what Garth wanted to hear. They were still talking when the door burst open and Candy flew in, clutching the ugliest, most miserable-looking cat Max had ever seen. An enormous but otherwise nondescript gray-striped cat with one torn ear and a crooked tail, it was curled up in Candy's arms like a baby. "I found him at the murder scene," she crooned. "Poor baby, somebody had deserted him and nobody would take him in— Did his stuff get here? Great. He hasn't had a thing to eat today except half of a rotisserie chicken. You guys talk while I get him settled in. I'm going to name him... Casanova!"

She scurried into her bedroom, dragging the bag of litter behind her. Garth and Blythe, who'd been hovering in the background wearing a cute little sundress and an inscrutable expression, exchanged a look Max didn't understand. Blythe said, "I don't think she needs Max anymore. Or me, for that matter."

Garth said, "I'm going to help her get Casanova settled in," and picked up the litter box under one arm and the bed under the other, then vanished into Candy's room.

Blythe looked at Max. "Do you understand Candy a little better now?" she said. Her eyes sparkled.

"No," Max said.

"She has a thing for stray cats," Blythe said.

SINCE CANDY REFUSED TO LEAVE Casanova to his own devices, Blythe cooked dinner at home, and over the course of the evening, they delicately, subtly changed partners. When Garth said he'd get a hotel room for the rest of his stay because Blythe had put in enough time on the sofa and Max heartily invited him to stay with him instead, and that *he'd* sleep on the sofa, Garth actually did say, "Thanks, old boy, but the hotel will be more comfortable for everybody."

While Candy and Garth were murmuring and laughing in one corner of the room, Max managed to say to Blythe, "If Candy sneaks out to Garth's hotel room in the middle of the night, give me a call."

The very thought sent another jolt of heat to the erection he'd been trying to hide all evening, and looking down at Blythe, so small, so perfect, he saw that her eyes had glazed over, her cheeks were flushed, her lips were swollen, her breasts heaved. The tiny tip of her tongue appeared and traveled slowly across her lower lip.

"Ah-h-h," he groaned.

"Uh-huh," Blythe whispered. "Me, too."

"If we're ever alone again, it's really going to be fun."

"A moment I shall eagerly await," she said, backing away just in time to keep him from beginning the moment at once.

BLYTHE LOOKED UP FROM HER desk the next afternoon to see Candy's head just barely poking around the thin wall of the cubicle. Candy usually just...appeared, not there one minute, filling the cubicle the next minute, so this hesitant approach was unusual. "Hi," Blythe said encouragingly. "Is Casanova still doing okay?"

"Garth checked on him at noon," Candy said. "Casanova scratched him, so I guess he's doing fine." She snaked around the corner. "I was just wondering," she said, "if you'd mind terribly if..."

"If..." Blythe prompted her.

"If Garth and I went out together this evening," Candy burst out all of a sudden, flopping down into the chair, her old self again. "It's his last night here and there are some things we'd like to talk about, you know, his family and my family and—"

"Of course I don't mind," Blythe said. Her curls were starting to twitch with anticipation. "You should spend some time together before he leaves."

"Are you sure you won't hate me forever if Garth and I get something going? I mean, I meant him for you, and he's so special, oh, Blythe, he's so much more special than Max." Candy was really on a roll now. "Max is a hunk and sweet as all get-out," she rambled on, "but he doesn't have Garth's education or emotional depth, and Garth is really, really rich, richer than my family. I mean, you'd never have to think about money again, and I just want to know if you're absolutely positive you don't want Garth for yourself?"

"Absolutely," Blythe said, struggling to keep her face straight, refusing to let herself add, "Second best is more than good enough for me."

"Actually," Blythe said, "Max and I might hang out together tonight. You and Garth can stay home with Casanova and give the guys a chance to bond."

She suddenly realized why Candy hunched over like that when she was having kind feelings for Blythe. She was getting herself down to Blythe's height. She'd been hunching over Casanova the same way when she brought him back to the newsroom. She was making an effort not to be intimidating. And Blythe also remembered why she was so fond of Candy, why she put up with her bullying, why she let Candy make a slave of her, simply because of moments like these when Candy let her true, tender self show.

"Thanks. That would be nice," Candy said. She gave Blythe one last pleading look. "Last chance," she said. "Are you sure?"

"Candy," Blythe said, "you and Garth were meant for each other, like yin and yang. His feet are firmly on the ground, and you can hold on tight to his hands while you fly."

Candy gazed at her thoughtfully. "That's beautiful," she said. "Did you make it up all by yourself?"

11

"GARTH JUST CALLED AND ASKED my permission to go out with Candy," Max said into the receiver. His voice was literally shaking with excitement.

"You granted it, I assume?"

"I said it was a tough one, but I'd think about it."

"You turkey!" He could hear the breathlessness in her voice. She must realize, as he did, what this development could do for their sex life. "I just had a visit of a similar nature. Candy gave me one last chance to keep Garth for my very own."

"You did say no."

"I said it was a tough one, but I'd think about it."

"You tart!"

"What are you doing tonight?" she said. Her voice had gone all low and throaty. Max felt the rush of heat to his groin.

"Having the hottest, heaviest sex of my entire career as a legendary sex object," he said.

"With anybody I know?"

"Ha-ha. Go straight to my apartment from work. No, go home and get clean towels first. Hell, I'll buy towels on my way back from City Hall. Get there as fast as you can. Do you even know my address?" He gave it to her. He gave her his cell phone number. As soon as he could have one made, he'd give her a key.

After he hung up the phone, he had a brief down

moment. He hadn't known her a week yet. It was much too soon to think about giving her his heart.

What was it about her that made him feel as if he'd known her forever, that they had some connection that was almost mystical?

Stupid as it was, he was thinking about pulling her right into his life.

A great time to make a major decision, right, Laughton? Stress of moving, stress of new job, stress of getting stuck in an elevator with no hope of rescue but a redheaded pixie with a comb, stress of being without all my stuff, my books, my CDs, hell, my damned coffeepot.

He reached over to the list he was making and wrote down "coffeepot, coffee, grinder, filters, cream, sugar" right under "towels," then added, "orange juice, bagels, cream cheese," gazed at the list and wrote down, "condoms."

Stress of being assigned a girlfriend by the girl you wanted to be your girlfriend, stress of being horny every second of the day and night, and not for the girlfriend you'd been assigned...

Yeah, terrific time for the big decision.

Better time to finish up his column and go shopping.

When the buzz came from the doorman at five-thirty, he was ready. Oh, more than ready. Blythe stepped into his apartment, looking fresh and bright-eyed, wearing a little sundress printed in the green of her eyes, her hair clean, shining and bouncy. He took her into his arms and just hugged her for a while.

"Finally," she said.

"No time schedule," he said.

"No Garth," she said.

"No Candy," he said. "Want to relax a while, have an early dinner and then fool around?"

"Let's fool around without dinner," she said.

"Wonderful idea," he said. He swept her up into his arms, loving her little shriek of surprise, carried her into the bedroom and dumped her unceremoniously into the center of the bed. Gripping the hem of his polo shirt, he pulled it over his head.

His cell phone rang while he was still tangled in his shirt. He groaned.

"Go on. Answer it," Blythe said softly from the middle of his bed.

He peeked out from under the shirt to see her shrugging the sundress off her shoulders. Under the sundress she was wearing a tight little white top, and her nipples pierced the fabric, taut and kissable.

Knowing he'd be sorry, he got one arm out of the shirt and picked up the phone.

"Smooth Moves at your service!" said Tiger Templeton. "We're parked right in front of your building and your porter's rolling out the plastic carpet. You ready for us?"

"You're here *now?*" Max felt stunned with disbelief. "It took you almost a *week* to get here from *Chicago* and *now* is when you show up?" He sent his horrified glance in Blythe's direction and found her all zipped up again and rolling around on his comforter, her face buried in one of his new pillows and gurgling sounds coming from her throat.

He put his hand over the receiver. "Blythe," he said sternly, "you don't seem to comprehend the *gravity* of the situation. My furniture has finally arrived. What are we going to *do?*"

"We're going to get you moved in," she snorted in what he thought was a pretty graceless way. "It's fate.

We're doomed. If you think about it, it's amazing you're not still in that elevator."

"LEAVE IT. I'LL DO IT in the morning," Max said when he saw Blythe, armed with his Swiss Army knife, approaching the pile of boxes in the middle of the floor with a look of purpose on her face. Tiger Templeton and his sidekick, Poky, had come and gone, richer by far than when they'd arrived, and Max was ready to go back to the exact point at which he and Blythe had been interrupted.

"Let's find the basics and unpack them," Blythe said so enticingly it was hard to resist her, but he did anyway, having a much stronger feeling of purpose.

"I have the basics. I have a bed, water, condoms and a credit card."

"Wouldn't you love to have some more towels?" she coaxed him. "A skillet? A teakettle? Clean clothes?"

"If we open the box of clothes I won't have to wash until next weekend," he admitted.

"Start reading labels," she said. "Oh, look, this one says Bathroom."

He sighed. "Okay, just the basics."

An hour later, she said, "Let's just order in Chinese. We're making such great progress, I hate to lose the momentum."

He hadn't lost any momentum while they unpacked. He still wanted to return to the part where Blythe was slipping off her sundress. But he got on the phone and ordered enough Chinese food for one quadrant of the Szechuan province.

She was a natural nester. There was no stopping her.

Blythe was as happy as a hummingbird on a hibiscus bush as she helped Max unpack the most necessary boxes and arrange his possessions in shelves and drawers. Making a home, her favorite thing to do. Okay, second favorite. While they ate take-out Chinese food straight from the boxes, she wondered how the future would unfold for her and Max. Now that Candy and Garth would be seeing each other as often as possible, Blythe would move into an apartment of her own to give them privacy. She knew it was time for her to move out of Candy's apartment. Would Max invite her to move in with him? She knew in her head it was much too soon for that, but her heart kept contradicting her. It was hard to sit back, adopt a wait-and-see philosophy, but that's what she would have to do. A day at a time. A minute at a time. And she had these minutes with Max. Who could ask for anything more?

Well, one thing more. As it turned out, there was time for more than moving him in. Pent-up desire gave the night its thrills and excitement. Knowing that at last they could take their time with each other, that they could throw guilt and responsibility out the window, made the night sweeter, deeper, richer and more sensually luxurious.

After completing the destruction of the bed by breakfasting there on bagels and cream cheese, they showered together, were forced to be severe with themselves about the necessity for going to work, and Blythe began to dress. She put on her favorite flowered skirt and coral T-shirt, the outfit she'd been wearing on the night she and Max met, and came back to the bathroom to get her hair under control and put on a little makeup.

"You packed a bag," Max said. "When did you do that?"

"When I went home to check on Casanova."

"How's he doing?"

"Great. Did I tell you he scratched Garth?"

"Smart cat."

"He tried to scratch me, too, but I was too fast for him. He trusts no one but Candy."

"No wonder he was abandoned."

"Max!"

He was shaving at the second sink and took a minute to swipe down one cheek before he said, unrepentant, "Hey, how would you like to take a little trip with me this weekend?"

"Where would I be going?" she asked him.

"My parents' fortieth wedding anniversary is this weekend. My sisters organized a big party—"

"I didn't know you had sisters. I don't know anything about you really. I wouldn't have known you had parents if—"

"Everybody has parents."

"Not everybody."

She thought she'd said it neutrally enough, but he put down his razor, wiped his half-shaved face and wrapped his arms around her. "I'm sorry," he murmured into her hair. "That was so thoughtless."

"It's okay," she said. "I shouldn't have reacted like somebody with a chip on her shoulder, because I don't have one, really, and of course I did have parents, I just don't have them anymore."

"I want to know everything about you," he said, rocking her in his arms. "Where you grew up, how you grew up..."

"And I want to meet your sisters." She ended the moment by backing off and giving him a mischievous smile. "I think I interrupted you in the process of inviting me to the anniversary party."

He gave her a little spank and went back to shaving. "Of course I was inviting you."

"Where do they live?"

"Butterfield, New Jersey."

"Is that why you moved to New York? To be closer to them?"

He mumbled something noncommittal.

"I'd love to go," she said.

"Great. We'll go Saturday and come back Sunday. That's enough family for one weekend. Oh..." He paused in his shaving. "When I tell Mom you're coming, she'll want to put us in separate bedrooms. She's that kind of person."

"The kind who believes that putting us in the same bedroom would be like saying, 'I know you're having sex,' and she likes to let people keep that sort of thing private if they want to?"

He put down his razor. "How'd you know?"

"I'm kind of like that myself," Blythe said.

She observed that he was giving her a seriously thoughtful look as he went into his bedroom to dive into his recently arrived clothes like a kid opening Christmas packages.

Soon after Blythe got to her desk, Candy barreled in. She'd obviously spent the night with Garth. First, she didn't mention that Blythe hadn't come home, and second, she was dressed exactly as she'd been dressed the day before, and the only makeup she was wearing was lipstick and mascara, which Blythe knew she carried in her handbag.

"He's gone," Candy said, and burst into tears.

"Not forever!"

"You think now until Friday night won't feel like forever?" Candy sobbed.

Now until noon would seem like forever if she couldn't get Candy calmed down. "Garth is coming back Friday?" she said. "See, he's really..."

"He invited me there. To Boston." Volatile as nitroglycerine, she stopped sobbing and started hyperventilating. "Oh, Blythe, I'm so scared. What can I do to make a good impression on him? Can you teach me to cook by Friday? Like really gourmet stuff. Garth's so knowledgeable about food—"

"Candy, Garth already knows you can't cook. He likes you even if you can't cook. Stop worrying."

"I need new underwear," Candy moaned.

"Can-deeeee..."

"Well, this is important," Candy said.

"I know," Blythe said, taking pity on her. "But you keep forgetting that he's just as crazy about you as you are about him. Just go to Boston and have fun."

Candy sat back, looking insecure. "You really think he's crazy about me?"

"I'm sure of it," Blythe said, and then asked her top-priority question. "What are you going to do with Casanova? Because I'm going to be away this weekend, too."

Candy stared at her. "I'm taking him with me, naturally. You don't adopt a cat and then just go off and leave him."

"Of course you don't," Blythe said. "What was I thinking?"

"Where are you going?"

"New Jersey," Blythe hedged.

"Have you had your shots?" Candy said.

It was an old New York joke, but Blythe laughed anyway.

"While I'm up in the Bronx," Candy said, "think about what can I do for Garth that would be so, so special..."

"While you do what in the Bronx?" Blythe said crisply. "Did the drug dealers reschedule their little get-together? Send you an e-mail notification, perhaps?"

"Don't be silly." Candy laughed and stood up. "I just have a hunch Maxie O'Conner's going to take out Big Boy Johnson one of these days and I want to go up and see if anybody has a little gossip to share. See you later."

She was back in two seconds. "Garth really didn't want me to go up to that neighborhood by myself," she said dreamily. "He's on the train to Boston, and he made me promise to call him every thirty minutes. He's so protective, so caring, so—"

"Sensitive?" Blythe said.

"Oh, yes," Candy said, and drifted away.

"I NEVER THOUGHT I'D SAY something this disloyal," Blythe groused as soon as she slid into the car Max had rented for the trip to New Jersey, "but I'm absolutely thrilled to have Candy out of my hair for a couple of days."

"She hasn't gone back to her old ways, has she?" Max said, frowning at her while she fastened her seat belt. "She didn't make you do her laundry or pack her bag or..."

The truth was that Blythe had helped quite a bit, a fact she decided not to share with Max because that, from her point of view, wasn't the problem. "She's been sweet as, well, as candy," Blythe said. "But she's a raving bundle of insecurities! Can you imagine Candy insecure? She's brought home and taken back four dinner dresses. She's prancing around the apartment modeling the underwear she's taking to Boston, for heaven's sake. She's so determined to cook breakfast for Garth Sunday morning that I had to teach her to make pancakes." It had taken her half the night to clean up the kitchen, too. And then she had to help Candy pack Casanova's travel kit. It had been like packing for a baby. She was so tired she was almost relieved that she and Max would be in separate bedrooms in his parents' house.

She gave him a sidelong glance. His smile was a flash of white teeth against his tanned face. His long, strong fingers held the steering wheel lightly and with confidence. She loved what his blue polo shirt did for his eyes, not that Max's eyes needed any help. His biceps bulged below the short sleeves, and—*oh, wow.* Observing the bulge in his spotless khaki pants, she fanned herself with the roadmap in the pocket of the passenger door.

"Want me to turn down the air?"

The temperature inside the car was in the sixties. Hers felt as if it had shot up above a hundred. "No, I'm fine," she said. "Okay, I'm through griping. Hi."

He reached over and took her hand. "Good morning to you, too."

She curved her hand around his and brought it to her lips, running her tongue down between his fingers, loving the low sound that came from his throat. "There's a Howard Johnson motel on Ninth Avenue," he said. "Watch yourself or we won't get any further than that."

"Don't tempt me. I have all the time in the world. You're the one with a schedule."

"Damn," he said, snatching his hand away just as she was about to capture one finger in her mouth and drive him wild.

Now that she was totally out of the mood to gripe about Candy, Blythe noticed for the first time that she was riding in a very luxurious sports car. "This is great," she said, patting the cream-colored leather upholstery. "What kind of car is it?"

"A Mercedes 600 SL."

"Wow." Expensive was the word that came to mind. Even expensive to rent.

"It's a new model. Twelve-cylinder. I wanted to try it out, because if I decide to park a car somewhere in the city, I might buy one of these."

Blythe had a moment of panic. She couldn't imagine being able to buy a car like this one. She'd understood that Max's father was a small-town newspaperman, but maybe the family was wealthy and snobbish and they'd look down on her in her discount-store sundress and sandals of no recognizable brand. "Are you absolutely sure it's okay with your mother for me to come with you?" she said, feeling about as insecure as Candy had been acting.

"Absolutely. The house has lots of room. She's looking forward to meeting you. So are my sisters. What Dad thinks about anything is a mystery."

Blythe smiled. "The strong silent type?" There was no way she could get out of meeting the Laughtons now. She might as well make the best of it.

"Yep."

"You mentioned sisters?"

"One older, one younger."

"It will be fun to see your family in action," she said wistfully.

He was silent for a moment, and then asked, "What was it like for you growing up?"

"Well, I—"

"You don't have to tell me if it makes you sad to talk about it."

His voice was so gentle, so kind. "We don't know anything about each other, not really," she said. "I'm about to meet your family, so I guess it's time I told you about me." She took a deep breath, getting ready for the long story she always dreaded telling. "I was just two when my parents were killed in the car wreck. We didn't have a big family. My grandmother was very sick and my aunt Cecile was getting a divorce, with two kids of her own to worry about. But some kind of family feeling was going on that kept them from being willing to put me up for adoption, so the alternative was foster homes."

"Plural? They kept moving you around?" Max sounded appalled. "What state are we talking about?"

"Southern Ohio, right on the Kentucky border," Blythe said. "But that's the way it's generally done. It's to keep the foster child and the foster family from developing too strong an attachment in case the birth family finds a way to take the child back. Mine didn't. Gramma died and Aunt Cecile remarried. I haven't heard from her in years. But I was okay. All my foster parents were kind to me."

"That's a relief," Max muttered. He reached over and squeezed her hand.

"My favorite foster home was the last one. The family lived on a farm," Blythe said, reliving the scent of new-mown hay and fresh-baked bread. "Rhonda, my foster mom, was really overworked, so I helped her when I got home from school. I liked being in the kitchen with her, harvesting vegetables from the garden and freezing or canning them, and I loved taking care of the two youngest kids. I could have stayed there in their town, gotten a job, married one of the local boys, but I—" She paused, remembering the agony of deciding whether to take the safe and easy path or opt for the scary and ambitious one. "I wanted something more."

AND THERE IT WAS, the clue to Blythe and what she wanted out of life. Bart had been right about her. Making a success of her life mattered desperately to her, because she had only herself to rely on.

While Blythe had been dealing with Candy's bout of insecurity, Max had been doing some deep thinking. He'd forced himself to admit that what he'd secretly wanted was the kind of home he'd grown up in, with one parent working hard at a paying job for the future of the family and the children's educations and the other one working just as hard at home to keep it running smoothly, to be there for the happy times and the tears and the fears and the incomprehensible homework.

It didn't matter which parent did which thing. He knew a couple of happy househusbands. The problem was that he couldn't see himself as a happy househusband. He'd play with the kids, sure. He got a kick out of playing with his niece and nephews, but there was more to child-rearing than play.

Like meals.

Most of all, he didn't see how he could be happy anywhere but in the newspaper business. Printer's ink, speaking figuratively, was in the family blood, handed down to him from his grandfather, then his father. Which meant Max had hoped to marry—if he married—a woman who wanted to do the at-home part of making a family. Now remembering what Bart had said about Blythe needing to succeed in a career, then hearing her say in her own words, *"I wanted something more,"* he realized she didn't intend to be that kind of wife.

Deciding she was worth a compromise on his part would take time. He reminded himself again that they'd only known each other a matter of *days*. It didn't seem possible. He felt he'd known her forever.

Even deep in thought, he was listening to what she was saying, murmuring responses, touching her hand or her shoulder when it was safe to take a hand off the steering wheel. He was trying to imagine how it would feel to be so alone in the world, and how she could sound so cheerful when she talked about it. She'd told him about getting a National Merit Scholarship and going to Wellesley. She was telling him how she still tried to keep in touch with her various foster parents, especially the family she'd left behind when she was eighteen to go out on her own. Yes, she'd wanted more and had had the courage to go out and find it.

Of course, some women changed after the kids came along. His older sister, Renee, for example, had quit her high-stress banking job and was happy at home with her children and volunteer work she could do at her own pace.

Some women did that, but you couldn't count on it. His younger sister, Polly, was a photojournalist, and while she'd quit buzzing around the world when her son, Paul, was born, she was still buzzing—around

New Jersey. Her husband was an artist, though, with a studio in the backyard, so Paul would never be without a parent to run to if he skinned his knee or had a falling-out with his best friend.

Max also had to remind himself that his sisters were financially secure. It made a difference.

He sighed. If he fell in love with Blythe, which he felt he was already doing, he'd have to love her just as she was. If she changed, he'd only love her more.

And...if what she wanted now was a better shake at the *Telegraph,* which she deserved, and an apartment of her own, where she could be independent from Candy's demands, he was doubly determined to help her get both those things.

"So Candy talked me into coming to New York with her, and here I am." Blythe was winding up. "Max, what are you doing?" she shrieked as he skidded across three lanes and onto an exit ramp.

"Almost missed our turn," he said, giving her a wicked grin as soon as he dared to take his eyes off the road. "Relax. You're in the hands of a master driver."

"You need a master navigator," she grumbled, pulling herself away from the door that his wild turn had pressed her against.

"Yeah," he said, "I do."

THEY REACHED BUTTERFIELD by a narrow, two-lane road. The town was small and charming, and Blythe gasped when Max wheeled into the driveway of a large white clapboard house shaded with trees, the fresh green lawn dotted with blooming shrubs and well-tended flower beds. It was so much like the house in her daydreams that for a second she thought she might be imagining it. The dark green door burst open and a swarm of Laughtons, she supposed, flew out.

"Get out of the car before we're trapped and suffocated," Max said, but in seconds he was inundated by hugs, kisses and laughter.

Blythe watched the scene with longing until she got that prickly feeling that she was being watched. She glanced down to find a little girl looking up at her. Not looking, glaring.

"Hi," Blythe said.

"Are you Uncle Max's new girlfriend?"

"I'm your uncle Max's friend, yes. I'm Blythe. What's your—"

"I used to be Uncle Max's girlfriend," the child said, "until *you* came along."

No sooner did she get Candy out of the running than her new competition showed up. "I have a feeling you'll always be your uncle Max's best girl," she said, smiling at her utterly beautiful competition.

"You got that right," Max roared, and swept the little girl off her feet. She shrieked with delight, her bad mood forgotten when he deposited a sloppy kiss on one cheek.

Blythe's attention was distracted by the youthful-looking woman in her sixties who was coming toward her. Slim and blond, she was dressed in beige slacks and an elegant white silk sweater set. Although she wasn't wearing an apron, she gave the impression that she'd just taken one off and was looking for someplace to dry her hands. Behind her, a man who looked like an older version of Max came along more slowly, a slight smile hovering around his mouth.

"Blythe," the woman said. "We're so glad you could come with Max. I hope we haven't frightened you. This family has no class." She paused for a swift, fond look around the group. "I'm Max's mother—call me Helena—and this is his father, Maxwell, Senior, and you've been talking to Priscilla, Renee's oldest..."

How could she ever remember all those names? Max's older sister Renee with her husband, Hilton, Priscilla's baby brother, whom they called Hill, then Polly and her bearded husband, Damon, with their two-year-old, Paul. She'd have to ask Max for a refresher course on the aunts and uncles.

"Come in and have lunch," Helena said. "We're having crab cakes, and I don't want them to get cold."

"Lunch was supposed to be my treat," Max protested.

Blythe glanced around. There appeared to be twenty or so people in the yard. A lot of people to treat.

"I canceled your reservation," Helena said primly. "This will be more fun." And she shooed them all into the house, where they squashed themselves around the long, rectangular kitchen table for the promised crab cakes, salads galore and homemade breads. A row of desserts sat on the kitchen counter beside them.

So this is what a happy home was like. Blythe was so overcome with the warmth of it that she felt like crying. But at this table, only laughing was allowed.

12

MAX WANDERED THROUGH the party, keeping an eye on Blythe to be sure she was having a good time. It was just like his mother to insist on having her fortieth-anniversary party at home. She'd let Renee and Polly have it catered, and might or might not end up letting the three of them pay for it, but neither the country club nor the resort hotel by the lake was her style, she'd said. Too sterile. Some of the friends she intended to invite might feel uncomfortable there.

Those friends were here right now, side by side with the newspaper staff and their neighborhood, town and country club friends, the woman who'd helped with the housekeeping for twenty years, patients from the AIDS clinic where his mother had been a volunteer for ten years, women she'd housed overnight when their husbands abused them.

In the dining room, where the table was loaded with the local caterer's choicest offerings, he sidled up to his father, with whom he'd had only a few words, as busy as he'd been keeping that little flirt Priscilla off Blythe's case and making sure Blythe wasn't being ignored.

Blythe had certainly not been ignored. His sisters had honed in on her like darts hitting the bull's-eye, and he hated to think what they'd been talking about. His mother had had plenty of time to talk to her, too, when Blythe was helping in the kitchen. He hadn't seen the photograph album come out, the one with the picture of him stark naked and peeing into a rhododendron bush, but who knew what secrets his mother *had* revealed?

"Good party, Dad," he said. This was typical of the deep and soulful conversations he and his father had. His father was a silent man, speaking mainly through the newspaper he loved so much. "Think you and Mom can patch things up and keep at it for another forty years?"

That netted him a grin. "It's been touch and go for the last month. The swivet that woman went into getting the house ready for this shindig was enough to drive anybody crazy. She decided the living room needed new curtains, so she made them."

"As extravagant as ever, huh?"

"Yep."

"Sorry Bart couldn't come," Max said. "I'm sure he told you Linda's mother had a stroke—"

"—and they flew to her deathbed. Ha. That woman will live to be a hundred ten, just to tick Bart off." Silence, then, "I like your girl."

Max hesitated. He still hadn't decided how he should bill his relationship with Blythe. Should he sink his head to his father's shoulder and announce weepily that he might be in love or downplay his feelings until a little more time had passed? "I haven't known her long. I mean, the year and a half I spent in that elevator only happened a week ago Thursday."

"All I said was I liked her."

"Well, so do I," Max admitted.

"Something about her reminds me of your mother."

It jolted Max. "She doesn't look anything at all like Mom. Mom's tall, blond..."

"I didn't say she looked like her," his father said patiently. "I said she reminded me of her."

That was what had been bugging Max all along. "You mean the way she never calls attention to herself? The way she sort of sneaks around taking care of other people?"

"Sneaks?"

"You know, like at lunch. I looked up and there was Blythe in the kitchen, scraping dishes and putting them in the dishwasher. I didn't even see her get up from the table." And the way she'd unpacked his boxes and put things away, making it look like a magic trick.

"Yeah, like that."

"No. She doesn't remind me of Mom," Max insisted. "I can't see her choosing the path Mom chose."

Of course, his mother had been totally secure about herself, about her intelligence, about her ability to support herself financially. That had made her choice easier. Blythe was a bundle of doubts and insecurities, and as Bart had said, she needed the financial security of a career as well as a clearer sense of her identity.

"I still like her," said his father.

"Well, thank you for admiring my taste in women. I..." He wondered if what he was about to say was too sentimental for Maxwell, Senior. He'd take a chance on it. "I admire yours, too," he said, and moved on to whirl Priscilla around the makeshift dance floor before things got any sappier.

"BLYTHE SEEMS LIKE A real sweetheart," Renee said a little later in the evening. "What's with you and her?"

"I haven't known her long." He needed to make up a new line.

"Long enough to bring her home to meet our parents," Renee teased him.

"Well, there was the party, and her roommate was out of town, and..."

"Sure. You didn't want her to be lonely. Yadda, yadda, yadda." She regarded him, her head cocked to one side. "You seem comfortable together."

"Yeah," Max said, "comfortable."

"Does she understand your financial situation?"

It would have seemed a crass question if Renee hadn't been moving up in an investments banking firm before she decided spending twenty-four hours a day with Priscilla was actually more challenging. "No," he said. "The topic's never come up. I guess she assumes I'm living on a newspaper columnist's salary." He thought about his apartment and its furnishings for a minute, the car he'd rented for the weekend. "Living pretty high on that salary, I guess."

"And she likes you anyway. Honest to God, women are such suckers for a pretty face." She gave him a friendly punch.

"Hey," he protested, "how do you know she's not a sucker for my brilliant columns?"

"Blythe is no sucker," Polly hissed, moving in on the sibling huddle. "She's just...nice."

SUNDAY AFTERNOON THE traffic was heavy. The Holland Tunnel was like Times Square on New Year's Eve, except that everybody was in a car and in a bad mood. Except Max. He was in a great mood, partly because Blythe apparently was, too.

"You have a wonderful family," she said with a deep sigh.

Max smiled. It was about the fifteenth time she'd

said that or something similar. She'd talked of nothing else on the drive home, asked questions about each family member, praised the children, applauded Renee and Polly, each for making her own choice about career versus home life. As for his mother, Blythe had waxed eloquent. "She and your dad are just crazy about each other," she said, "and he's terrific. He didn't talk much, but he just smiles in that nice way that says, 'Everybody have fun, just don't make me join in.'"

"That sure hits the nail right on the head," Max said. "How'd you figure that out so fast?"

She was quiet for a moment. "Just by watching," she said.

If all the raving about his family had come from anybody else—although, darn it, he did have a pretty neat family as families went—he would have been calling it empty flattery by now and suspected that the person doing all the raving had a secret agenda. But even before she said, "Just by watching," he'd known that in the family setting, Blythe must have felt she'd been put down in a fantasy world, and she was only trying to figure out the rules and the players.

His heart went out to her. He wasn't sure if he wanted to marry her or just give her his family.

"Oh," Blythe said suddenly, "I forgot to tell you. Sacha wants to write a story about you and Candy and Garth and me. I can't imagine what she finds interesting about our lives, can you?"

Max laughed.

He laughed to cover up the serious thoughts that were going through his mind. He'd received Blythe's message loud and clear. Blythe wanted more. *More* meant career and her own apartment and freedom to choose whether to marry and whom to marry.

He'd hoped... But if that was what she wanted, then he was the guy to help her get what she wanted.

BLYTHE WAS CURLED UP IN BED, luxuriating in Max's arms, warm and tingly with anticipation of a night of intense and glorious sex, when the phone rang.

Max's sigh was deep and meaningful. "It's a conspiracy," he said.

"Go on. Answer it," she encouraged him. "It might be important. I'm not going anywhere."

Max growled, but he reached for the cell phone, still his only means of communication. "Candy!" he said, sitting up abruptly. "How was your weekend? Sure, I'll put her on." He waggled his eyebrows at Blythe and handed her the phone.

"I thought you'd be there," Candy said to Blythe. She was breathless with excitement. "I hope I'm not interrupting anything. I have such incredible news I couldn't wait until morning."

"Give me a second to untie Max," Blythe said, "and put my whips away."

"What?"

"Blythe!" Max said.

She blew a kiss at him. "Okay, he's loose now," she said. "What's happened?"

"Garth and I...well, Garth wants us to be together."

"Well, yes. We know that."

"No, I mean *together*, like together in the same city and the same apartment all the time."

"It must have been the pancakes," Blythe said, smiling at Max as she trailed a hand down his chest, making circles in the crisp, dark hair. "I'm so happy for you, Candy." And she truly was. She and Garth might be the only people in the world who knew Candy was like a pair of brass knuckles with a heart of gold. "Are you moving to Boston?"

"No," Candy said on a deep sigh. "That's the incredible part. Garth knows how much my career matters to me. He's going to phase out his practice in Boston and start one here."

"Wow," Blythe said. "He really loves you, Candy."

"I think he must," Candy said, and hesitated.

Blythe caught her cue. "He'll move in with you, then, so of course I'll move out. I'll—"

"I feel bad about that part of it, and I'll help you with the move," Candy said. "On the other hand, this may be all it takes to get Max to ask you to move in with him."

Max was hanging over her shoulder, anxious to hear the news. "Oh. Well," Blythe said. She kept her voice neutral, but her heart was singing with hope. "I'll talk to you about that tomorrow."

"Casanova let Garth feed him some smoked salmon and didn't even try to scratch him, didn't even hiss," Candy said, dreamy again. "We've hurdled a major barrier."

"What happened?" Max said at once when she'd handed him back his phone.

"Garth's giving up his practice in Boston to be with Candy," Blythe said, "and Casanova's given his stamp of approval. Is that true love or what?"

"Wow," Max said. He gathered her into his arms again and held her close. "Happy as I am for Candy," he murmured into her hair, "I'm happier for us. Candy's all taken care of and we don't have to think about anybody but ourselves. Now's the time to..."

Blythe's heart raced. Now's the time for us to move in together? Now's the time for us to think about getting married? No, no, too soon. Now's the time to say, "I think I love you, and what are we going to do about it?"

She'd settle for a simple statement of that sort for now, because that's where she stood at the moment. She knew she was wild about him, knew she was crazy for his kisses, his body consuming hers, but it was also possible that what she was feeling was a lasting kind of love.

She could see herself settling into that family of his and finding a home at last. But getting a ready-made family wasn't what it was all about. It was all about Max himself, and she still had a lot to learn about him. Now that she'd met his family, she knew he could be the man who would respect her for being willing to quit her job, give up her career prospects, in order to make a happy home for him and their children. All she needed to be sure was...time.

MAX WAS THINKING HOW MUCH he wanted to say, "Now's the time for us to move in together," but he knew Blythe wanted more and he'd promised himself he'd help her realize her dreams. Moving directly from Candy's overpowering personality to his—because she hadn't had a chance to see how driven he could be when he'd gotten hold of some interesting or scandalous or provocative information and intended to write about it—wouldn't give her a chance to set her own agenda and follow it.

First Blythe had to figure out who she was and whether she could live with the person he was.

Damn, I sure do sound mature, don't I? Just like Garth. Bleahh.

So instead of saying, "Now it's time for us to get married, move to a nice burb with good schools and have a couple of kids after you finish decorating," because money wouldn't be a problem, and there was nothing standing between the two of them and that outcome except that little matter of barely knowing each other, he said, "Now's the time for you to break out of your rut at the *Telegraph*, show Bart what you can do. Once you're in your own apartment and independent from Candy, the sky's the limit." He hugged her tight, hoping she wouldn't decide she wanted to be totally independent from him.

BLYTHE FELT HERSELF slow down inside, felt her emotions grind to a halt. Disappointment, thick and dark, welled up inside her, unfairly she knew, but there nonetheless. Max wanted a successful, independent career woman after all.

Without opening her eyes, she let her mind scan his apartment. While it wasn't all that large, it was in a prime Upper West Side location, in a prewar building that had twelve-foot ceilings. His furniture was high-quality contemporary, Italian design, expensive. He had the latest in computer equipment, sound equipment and not merely one flat-screen television set but two.

As a bachelor, he lived well on the unspectacular salary of a newspaper columnist. Maybe too well. For all she knew, he might be deeply in debt. To add another person to his responsibilities, he'd want the safety net of a second salary to support his lifestyle.

This shook her. Whether it was a highly successful

career woman he wanted or a woman whose net worth made it unnecessary for her to worry about bringing home a salary, she was not the person to fill the bill. She didn't aspire to great wealth, but maybe he did.

Now that they could be together without conniving and had time to confront the practical aspects of a relationship, maybe they weren't right for each other after all. Sometimes people changed, but she couldn't count on Max to change. She'd have to take him—or not get him—exactly as he was.

"I'll start looking for an apartment immediately," she said. Her voice wavered a little.

"Not immediately," he said, his low, warm voice surrounding her like melted chocolate. "First we have to attend to these..."

Blythe shivered as he dipped his head to her bare breasts and ran his tongue in a circle around one instantly puckering nipple.

"...and this..."

She lay back, willing herself to enjoy the moment. Any one of these moments might be the last.

"...and this."

"I'll start tomorrow," she moaned, arching her back and letting her sadness and anxiety dissolve in the pleasure of his caresses and the promise of the ultimate pleasure of sheltering him inside her.

"I'LL TALK TO SACHA TODAY," Blythe said while they rushed around Max's apartment trying to make it to the *Telegraph* offices before they were noticeably, embarrassingly late. "She might have some ideas about where to look for apartments. She might even be getting a bigger place with her advance money. I could rent her apartment."

She was getting pretty tired of sounding so determinedly cheerful. Not that she wasn't excited about moving out of Candy's apartment. Not that she wouldn't have loved to have had Sacha's cozy little place—before she met Max and decided the only home she could bear was one with him in it.

"May I help you look?" Max's tone rang false, as if he were trying to sound determinedly cheerful himself, and she wondered why. Probably because he didn't enjoy househunting but felt obligated to help.

"No need to tie up your time," she told him. "I may need to look at tons and tons of places before I decide. You'll get bored."

"No, I won't." He no longer sounded determinedly cheerful. He just sounded determined. "We'll buy a second paper and both of us can go through the classifieds. Or we can consult an apartment agent."

"Is that how you found this apartment?"

"Yes."

"Isn't there a huge fee for using an agent?"

"Yes."

"I'll see if I can find one by word of mouth," Blythe decided.

"I'll ask around," Max said. Now she observed a tightness around his mouth she hadn't noticed before. "You want something nice."

"No, I want something cheap," Blythe said.

"No sacrifice too great when the reward is independence."

She gave him a sharp look. He was the one who'd said she should look for an apartment. What was the business about sacrificing for independence all about? "Ready to go?" she said, afraid they were about to slip into fighting mode without her even knowing what they were fighting about.

"All set. I'll come by your desk at five, five-thirty, and we'll share information."

"Sure. I'll call Sacha."

MAX WENT DIRECTLY TO Bart's office when he'd left Blythe at her desk, still checking through the classifieds and crowing about the possibilities. "Bart, you've got to do something about Blythe," he said.

Bart blinked. "What? Adopt her?"

Max snorted and pawed the floor. "No. She's over-educated and underemployed, and I want you to upgrade her job."

Bart sighed. "Max, she's just not a reporter at heart. She doesn't have that killer instinct Jacobsen has."

"Then why'd you hire her?"

"I'd already hired Jacobsen, and Jacobsen said I'd be sorry if I didn't hire Padgett. I wasn't sure what she meant by that. Like, maybe she had mob connections and if I didn't hire Padgett, they'd find me at the bottom of the Hudson sealed inside a car with Jersey tags. So I hired her. Luckily she's a great copy editor."

Max flung his hands up in the air. "Is there anybody who isn't afraid of Candy?"

"No." Bart seemed quite sure of it. "Padgett might be better off writing features," he went on, "but I'm not the features editor."

Max was sure he'd feel really bad in the future if he got Bart by the throat, but thought it might feel really good right now. "So. Move. Her. To. Features," he said through clenched teeth.

"They don't have any openings."

"Make one."

"Fire somebody?"

"No. Just…do something."

Bart sighed again. "Okay, okay…"

"In the meantime," Max said, moving on inflexibly, "consider sending Candy out to get the facts and Blythe to write the stories. Make them a team." He tensed his muscles and rose a little in his chair. "And raise Blythe's salary to match Candy's."

"*A-a-rr-gh,*" Bart moaned.

"How's Linda's mother?" Max said next.

"*A-a-rr-gh,*" Bart moaned again.

"I take it she's fine," Max said. "I'm so happy for you."

"SACHA? BLYTHE. I wanted to ask you…"

"I've got some waivers here for you four to sign," Sacha interrupted her. "My editor says you have to."

"I don't think we've thought over the matter of being in your book," Blythe said. "What I called about was…"

"You have to let me tell your story!" Sacha sounded almost tearful. "Blythe, this book is going to be so funny, much funnier than the first one, and I made all that up, but it will be sweet and touching, too. 'A story to make you laugh and cry,' they'll say in *Publishers Weekly.*"

"If it gets to the point of being reviewed by *Publishers Weekly,*" Blythe said, "I will certainly buy a copy. But—"

"You can't let me down." Sacha had given up on tears and was down to using a low, pathetic groan. "I have to follow up the first book with a better one. I'm buying an apartment!"

"*That's* what I called about," Blythe said. "Your apartment."

"You want my apartment?"

"Yes, or one like it," Blythe said. "Candy and Garth are a serious item now. I guess I should have let her tell you herself, but—"

"She did," Sacha said. "She's told everybody. We went to lunch. She told the waiter and some total strangers at the next table. But she thought, well, she and I both thought that maybe you'd, ah—"

"Move in with Max?" Blythe said, recreating the old determinedly cheerful voice. "Oh, no, much too soon," she said as if Sacha should have known better. "Remember, Candy has known Garth all her life. I've only known Max since the lights went back on."

Just since the lights went back on. It seemed like a lifetime. She found it hard to remember what life was like without Max. It was unbearable to imagine a future without him and to confront the possibility that she might be looking at exactly that—a future without Max.

13

"CAN'T YOU STAY WITH MAX while Garth is here this weekend?" Candy wanted to know when she tracked Blythe to her cubicle and found her calling small, inexpensive hotels.

"I probably can, but I don't want to start taking it for granted," Blythe said.

"I'd think he'd be hot to have you there." Candy's eyes held a teasing glint, but a slight frown of worry said she had something on her mind that didn't amuse her at all.

"We'll see," Blythe said. "You just enjoy your weekend. I'll be fine."

Candy hesitated. "You and Max haven't..."

"Oh, no," Blythe assured her. "In fact, I'm seeing him right after work."

"Good." The frown faded.

"To look for an apartment for me."

Candy's frown came back. "You're sure that's what you want to do?"

"Yes, of course," Blythe said. "It's exactly what I want to do." As Candy handed over a story for rewriting and left, Blythe observed that her frown had deepened alarmingly.

"SACHA WANTS ME TO TAKE a look at her apartment," Blythe told Max that afternoon when he appeared in the doorway of her cubicle. "She says I need to see it with the eyes of a person who's actually thinking of living there."

"I'll go with you."

"Are you sure you..." Since he was whisking her out the door, it appeared that he was going with her whether he wanted to or not.

The apartment was in Chelsea. Blythe walked up the steps and pushed the button for Sacha's apartment. Sacha's voice came from the speaker almost immediately, harsh and scratchy, and a buzz came from the door.

"No doorman," Max said as he pushed the door open.

"You knew that. You were here." She followed his long, rapid stride down the hallway to the elevator.

"What if she hadn't answered? There you'd be, out on the steps, and what if a mugger came along while you were standing here, or a rapist?"

Blythe gazed at him for a moment. "Well, this afternoon in the bright hot sunshine you were with me to protect me from the muggers and rapists. If I lived here, I'd be safe inside while a friend of mine was getting mugged or raped, which would be most unfortunate, but unlikely in the bright hot sunshine. I guess I could say, 'No admittance after sunset,' then nobody would get mugged or raped on my account."

"It's not safe," Max said stubbornly, and punched the button for Sacha's floor.

All Blythe knew was that the minute the way was cleared for Max and her to be together, he'd changed. He didn't want her anymore. It was a struggle to keep from crying, had been all day. She didn't know how to fix whatever might have gone wrong. She was already doing what he'd told her to do—look for an apartment. What else did he want from her? A Pulitzer Prize for covering an important story?

Sacha greeted them warmly. "I put the forms out here, on the dining table, just in case you—"

"What forms?" Max said.

"We'll talk about it later," Blythe said hurriedly. "Let's look at the apartment and let Sacha get on with her life."

"You understand," Sacha said anxiously, "that I haven't bought an apartment yet. It might be three months, six months."

"That long," Blythe said.

"Easily. It's not like it's going to happen this week. It's even possible I might chicken out. For example," she added pointedly, "if I can't get a proposal accepted fast enough for the next book." Her face cleared and she became a sympathetic friend again. "I know what you're worried about. Candy and Garth are planning to spend the weekends together until he's ready to start up a practice here. But don't worry about it. You can stay with me anytime Garth is around." Now she sent a pointed look at Max.

"Blythe will stay with me when Garth is in town," he said.

"Good. That's taken care of then," Sacha said.

No, it wasn't! How could she stay with Max, even tonight, when he was in this strange, distant mood?

"Have much of a problem with roaches?" Max asked Sacha.

"Not much," Sacha said.

"How about rats?"

"Max!" Blythe couldn't believe he was being so rude.

"These are things you need to know." Max was still wearing that stubborn expression. "How much is your electric bill? Gas bill? Is the apartment quiet enough that you can sleep?"

He gave Sacha a good, long look, hoping she'd act just as smart as she had on the night of the party and figure out that he didn't want Blythe to rent her apartment—any apartment, for that matter. Because he was getting a stronger and stronger feeling that he'd gone about this business of where Blythe should live all wrong.

He didn't want her living in a separate apartment. He wanted her with him. He wanted to protect her and take care of her and support her so that it wouldn't matter what her salary was at the *Telegraph*. He'd assumed, and he'd probably been right, that she wanted a term of independence first. But why hadn't he asked her what she wanted instead of making a unilateral decision?

What had he thought she was going to do when he suggested she get her own apartment? Say, "I don't want my own apartment. I want to move in with you"? Blythe was too unsure of herself to say anything like that. The invitation would have to come from him, and instead of inviting her, begging her, pleading with her, he'd blown it.

So it was too soon. Who cared? Living together was the best way to find out if they were right together. If they weren't, he'd buy her an apartment when they broke up, give it to her outright.

Just thinking about "breaking up" with Blythe made a big lump in his throat. And from Sacha's fixed and frowning gaze, he gathered that she wasn't going to help him out again, probably didn't trust him anymore because he hadn't asked Blythe to move in with him. He swallowed hard, still looking at Sacha, and saw her expression alter.

"As a matter of fact," she said, raising an eyebrow, the one Blythe wouldn't be able to see, "you never have to worry about the roaches for long, because when enough residents have complained, the super has the building exterminated. I don't *think* we have rats." She cocked her head to one side. "I *think* the scrabbling sounds I hear in the ceiling are just the neighbor's cat using her litter box. It isn't often bad enough to keep me awake. Just three or four nights a week. And this building is so safe!" She looked proud. "Only eleven unprovoked attacks on residents in the four years I've been living here."

Blythe's eyes went round. "I probably should look at a few other apartments before I make a final decision," she said. "I might find one I could move into a little faster."

"Of course," Sacha said. "It's the only sensible thing to do. But you'll love this place once you're in it. Go take a look at the bathroom before you leave. Try the water. We usually have hot water."

When Blythe scurried into the bathroom, Sacha turned to Max. "That's the last break I'm giving you, dumb-ass."

Blythe scurried right back. "Does the water always make that fingernail-down-the-blackboard sound when you turn it on?"

"Always," Sacha said, again with pride. "You can depend on it."

Max was grateful to her for rescuing him one more time. But what in the world did she mean by calling him a dumb-ass?

"We'll go up to the meatpacking district for dinner," he said as he ushered an oddly silent Blythe out of Sacha's building.

"Those restaurants are so expensive," she said. "Couldn't we—"

"My treat."

"You shouldn't be spending your money like this, on dinners out. You should be saving for your future."

"I am saving for my future. Doesn't keep us from having a decent dinner."

Now she *really* sounded like his mother.

"COME OVER AND TALK TO ME a minute."

Hearing Bart's voice, Blythe clutched the galley proof she'd been correcting to her chest, instinctively tensing up. In the early days, when Bart had hated every story she'd brought in, she'd dreaded picking up the phone and hearing his voice. They hadn't had one of those little talks in a long time. She must be succeeding at proofreading and rewrites.

She stood up, still going over the possibilities. Maybe she wasn't succeeding, or she was but the paper was going broke and downsizing, and of course, she'd be the first person Bart would lay off. Let go. Fire. She was having this conversation with herself. She might as well be blunt.

She drooped through the newsroom and knocked on his door.

"Padgett," he said by way of greeting. "Sit down."

He seemed even sadder than usual, a bad sign. "I'm raising your salary," he said.

It came as a shock. But as depressed as Bart looked, screaming, "Yippee" and doing a double cartwheel would have been like laughing at a funeral. "Thank you, Bart," she said with what she hoped was the right show of pleasure and gratitude without the hoopla. "That's very kind of you."

"You're going to go out with Jacobsen to get a story, and then come back and write it while she noses out some more news for herself. You'll be a team, like Danny DeVito and Arnold Schwarzenegger."

Blythe smothered the giggle that was rising in her throat.

"So your salary will advance to her level."

He might need life support before he finished telling her the good news.

"Until they find a spot for you in Features."

"Features?" Blythe said. Her spirits rose even higher. "You're going to move me up to Features?"

"Home decor," Bart said, pronouncing it "day-core." "Do good, you might end up being Homes Editor. But don't go out and buy a yacht, because we have to get you on the staff first."

"I don't know what to say." Blythe suddenly felt a little weepy herself. "I'm flattered, and honored... I know I'd be better at writing features than news. I won't embarrass you on the sixth floor, I promise."

Bart hung his head and mumbled.

"I'll let you get back to work, then," she said, still holding back on the "Yippie" and the cartwheels, then realized the downside of her good fortune. "Have you talked to Candy?"

"Yeah."

"Is she okay with it?"

He looked up, surprised. "Sure."

She smiled, feeling at last content with what was happening in this corner of her life. Sacha couldn't be happier with her huge advance than Blythe was with her meager raise and the future promise of work she might actually enjoy and do well. Since Max filled the other three corners of her life and things weren't going well there at all, it wasn't a total turnaround, but it helped.

Back in her office, forcing herself to settle down to work, she couldn't find the galley proof she'd been working on and realized that in her nervousness about what Bart might be about to tell her, she'd taken it with her.

She went swiftly back to his office, heard him talking on the phone and silently eased the door open. He had turned his back to her while he carried on his conversation. The galleys had to be in the second visitors' chair. She could grab them and run without disturbing him.

"I just gave her the news, Max," Bart said as she grabbed for the sheaf of papers. "You'd better be right."

She was out the door, the galley crushed to her chest again. She had to get back to her cubicle before she burst into tears. She was getting a raise, she was sharing the recognition with Candy, she was on the waiting list for a job in Features because Max had asked Bart to do those things for her. Max, who had known Bart since infancy and knew Bart would help him out if he could.

The fact that she hadn't gotten them because she deserved them didn't seem to matter at all right now. What mattered was the confirmation that Max wanted her to be a more successful person with a higher salary before he could give any more of himself to her.

Right before her eyes, her dream of being a dedicated wife and mother, the kids cramming into the station wagon, the sexy, loving husband who would kiss her goodbye...all that fell off the George Washington Bridge and drowned ignominiously.

Until that moment when it did, she didn't realize how much it meant to her. Succeeding in the marketplace meant a consistently tensed-up tummy, a feeling of being torn between home and office, and worst of all, children like the offspring of several of her and Candy's married friends, children who didn't seem to know which caretaker, their mother or their nanny, to call Mamma.

Blythe knew in her heart that her mother, while she lived, must have been with her almost constantly because, however kind Rhonda and her foster mothers had been to her, she'd never stopped missing the mother she'd lost.

In fact, she was missing her now, and the pain was so sharp that her loss might have happened yesterday. She sank her head to her desk and gave in to the tears she'd been holding back, tears for what she'd lost, tears for what might have been, tears for what she thought she'd found and felt now she'd never have.

So what she had to decide now was whether Max—just as he was—was worth giving up her dream.

"WHAT DID I DO THAT MADE her turn me down?" Blythe said to Max after they'd toured three apartments, one of which she'd been prepared to rent on the spot until the owner of the narrow town house in the Village had suddenly said she might not want to rent to a single person after all.

"Want to sue her?" Max said. "I'd be happy to find you a lawyer."

Right. Spend wildly and find a woman who can cover your bills.

"No. I'll just keep looking."

"I'll keep helping," Max said. "I'm sort of getting into this real estate thing. But now..." And right there in Cherry Lane, in front of God and everybody, he captured her in his arms and hugged her tight. "Now we're going to have a big blowout at Babbo to celebrate your promotion."

"You can't get reservations at Babbo at the last minute, not at eight o'clock."

"I did. Come on, *Miz* Padgett," he said, emphasizing the "Ms." "Time to celebrate."

It was Wednesday. Garth would arrive in the first flush of admitted love for Candy on Friday. She had two days to decide whether to spend the weekend with Sacha or with Max. She was sure the food at Babbo on Waverly Place was wonderful, not that she could remember a mouthful of it.

Pleading a champagne-induced migraine, she told Max she'd like to go back to Candy's, although she puzzled over the look in Max's eyes when she announced her intention to do just that.

"Oh, God, I'm so frigging glad you're here," Candy said when Blythe walked through the door of the apartment. "Let's go."

"Where? Why?"

"Who, what and when," Candy said. Her eyes were gleaming. "This is going to be great, Blythe, us working together as a team. We have to get up to the Bronx. The Yankees are planning to take out the Mets. We have to be there first and get the story."

"We're going to a baseball game?" Blythe said,

amazed at Candy's lack of jealousy in regard to her promotion. "Candy, it's late, it's after eleven."

"Gangs," Candy said with unusual patience. "It's a gang war. One gang calls itself the Yankees, so the other one calls itself the Mets. I've been working on this one for weeks. Now that you're here to write the story, I can throw myself into the fray." She shoved Blythe across the hall to the elevator.

Blythe found herself on a subway, speeding north to the Bronx. Next she found herself in a neighborhood that appeared to have barricaded itself in for the night. And next—

"What's the issue here?" Candy was saying to a man—a boy, really.

"Nunnayorbizness," he said. "Get outathuway. No place for a lady. Bad stuff's comin' down."

"I'm not a lady. I'm a reporter," Candy persisted. Blythe slowly edged up to the confrontation, holding a notebook and a pen, and heard Candy's cell phone ringing at the same time she heard gunfire. She ducked. Candy didn't, just moved forward, thrusting her cell phone at Blythe and crisply ordering her to "Answer it!"

Blythe did as she was told. "Where has Candy dragged you off to?" It was Max's voice, dear and safe, but loud. "Why aren't you at home where you belong?" he yelled at her. "What am I hearing? Guns? Blythe, where the hell are you? What were you thinking? Don't you give a damn about us? About our future?"

Shots rang around her ears, so she scooted toward the curb and crouched down low behind a rusted car. "What future?" she said. "Don't you want me to be a career woman? Didn't you force Bart to advance my career? Well, this is it, Max, advancement. Bye. I'm covering a gang war." She ended the call.

She edged up toward Candy, who was miraculously still standing, slung an arm around her waist, and with superhuman strength fired by sheer terror, dragged her down behind the parked car. The cell phone rang again, and while she kept a stranglehold on Candy, she answered it.

"Where are you?" It was Max again, sounding grim.

"I haven't the faintest," she said, and hung up.

It rang again. "Give me the frigging phone," Candy muttered and snatched it away from Blythe. "We're at..." she gave Max the cross streets "...and if you tell Garth about this you'll never write another column for the *Telegraph*, get it, buster?"

MAX HAD GOTTEN IN A TAXI seconds after his first call. Now he gave the driver the cross streets and then said to Candy, who was on the phone, "You let anything happen to Blythe and..."

She didn't let him finish his threat. "*This* wouldn't be happening to Blythe if you weren't such a dumb—Gotta go."

"Hurry!" Max yelled at the driver. Candy had been about to call him a dumb-ass. Second woman who'd called him one this week.

He arrived at the scene to find flashing lights, police cars, fire trucks, ambulances and Candy right in the middle of it all. Panicked, he searched for Blythe and eventually found her sitting in the back seat of a police car. He threw open the door, lunged for her and took her in his arms. She was limp and unresponsive. His heart sank all the way down to his loafers.

"You could have gotten shot jumping into the car

like that," she said in a preternaturally calm voice. "I'm under police protection."

If he couldn't hug her, he still had to touch her. He cupped her face in both hands and looked into her eyes. They were expressionless. "What's wrong?" he said gently. "I mean, between you and me."

"There can't be a you and me," Blythe said and ended with a little sigh. "I can't do this, Max. I probably won't even be good enough at home decor to be the kind of career woman you're looking for. I'll never make the kind of money you want the woman you marry to be making. I just want—"

His hands froze around her face. He couldn't seem to move. "What are you saying about money?"

"Oh, Max, I can tell you're living beyond your means. I can't live that way. I chose a profession that doesn't pay particularly well because I love that profession—parts of it, anyway—but the job I'd really like to do doesn't pay anything—not in dollars, anyway. So we wouldn't be happy together."

He listened, stunned, trying to put together the pieces of what she was saying. Slowly he took his hands away from her face. She turned her head and stared blankly out the window at the police activity.

He finally knew what she wanted.

"This isn't the time to make a final decision about anything," he said, keeping his voice low and quiet, not wanting to scare her. "Take a couple of days to think things over. Then we'll talk when we're both clearheaded."

She just nodded.

He hung around at a distance until he saw Candy climb into the front seat of the car, followed by a burly cop who was apparently going to drive them home. He snagged a ride to the subway from another team of cops. About Blythe, he was scared but not defeated.

He'd done it again. He'd gotten his love life in a mess because he hadn't come right out and said what was on his mind and, worse, hadn't given Blythe a chance to tell him what was on her mind. But it was different this time. This time it was of maximum importance to fix the mess he'd made, and furthermore, he knew how to.

He *thought* he knew how to. He *hoped* he knew how to. Because he had to fix it.

Marathon Man was what he was calling himself when he reflected on what he managed to accomplish in the next week. He wrote his columns, learned how to wash clothes in the basement laundry room, made appointments with both Candy and Sacha so they could yell at him about how badly he'd misread Blythe, confessed to Bart that he'd sabotaged Blythe's getting that last, suitable apartment by confiding in the owner of the building that Blythe would need to practice on her drums at least four hours a day, from 8:00 p.m. until midnight. His other projects took the most time, though. By Friday week, he was ready.

BLYTHE WAS SLUMPED OVER her keyboard writing the last follow-up story on the shootout between the Yankees and the Mets when the phone rang, and it was Max on the other end of the line. "Can we talk?" he asked her.

"I guess. I don't know what we have to talk about."

The sound of his voice drove out what little peace of mind she'd achieved in a week without him. She felt her body waking up, her heart pounding, her pulse racing—all for nothing. She'd learned a hard lesson. Next time, she'd find out everything about the guy before she fell head over heels in love with him. She wasn't dealing well with heartbreak, not eating, not sleeping, just walking around feeling like the living dead. It would pass. It had to. She couldn't keep functioning in a coma.

Candy was trying to be comforting, but those occasional lapses into starry-eyed anticipation of Garth's arrival reminded Blythe too keenly of what she herself might have had. She was spending another weekend with Sacha. Her bag was packed and sitting in the corner. Sacha would make her feel better.

Max was still talking, telling her they had lots to talk about, and she tried to tune back in to what he was saying. "I'll pick you up at the Forty-fourth Street entrance at five," he was finishing up.

"Okay," she said. "I'll have to bring my suitcase so I can go straight to Sacha's apartment after we talk. Garth's coming back to town."

A few minutes before five o'clock, she was on the sidewalk with her small rolling bag. Max wasn't there yet, which was fine. She needed those few minutes to compose herself. A white Land Rover pulled up to the curb. She gave it an idle, one-second lookover. Nice car. The kind she'd hoped to fill with Max's children. Tears came to her eyes and she blinked them back. She heard a honk. The man in the car was waving to her. *No, thanks, I don't need a ride, and you don't fool me with that innocent-looking family car, either.* She leaned down to frown at him through the window.

The man was Max.

Feeling suddenly heavy and clumsy, she went toward the SUV. Max leaped out, looking disgustingly healthy, rested and cheerful, grabbed her bag, tossed it in the back seat and herded her into the front seat. He pulled away from the curb just ahead of the policeman who was zeroing in on him for parking illegally, got through the intersection before the light turned red, then gave her a sidelong glance and a mischievous smile.

It was amazing how much happier he seemed now that they'd broken up.

"Why are we driving to look at the apartments?" she asked him, not smiling back.

"To try out my new car."

She shot him a surprised look. "I thought you were going to buy that little sports car."

"I was, but then I decided that this would work better for me."

"Oh." A Land Rover was expensive enough, but at least it wasn't a Mercedes—whatever. The way he spent money would have driven her crazy.

"And I found a place you might want to live."

"Really?" He just couldn't give up, could he? "I thought you understood I'd be planning my own life from now on."

"You will, you will." He hummed the words.

She didn't worry when he started up the Henry Hudson Parkway. It was one way to get to the Upper West Side where he lived, where many people lived. When he didn't take the Riverside Drive exit, she did start to worry.

"Where are we going?"

"You'll see."

He took the Cross County Parkway and she got truly nervous. "I don't want to live out this far. I like being close to work."

"Just hold on." He punched a button and a CD began to play a Beethoven concerto. "Want something to drink?" he asked her. "Look in the red cooler."

The cooler was filled with iced-down diet colas. She got out one for each of them, and when she was facing forward again, they were on the Hutchinson Parkway and speeding north into Connecticut.

"Okay, that's it. Turn around," she ordered him. "I don't want to live in the suburbs. I can't afford to live in the suburbs. I'd have to take a train into town. I'd have to pay New York taxes *and* Connecticut taxes. I'd have to have a car to go to the grocery store. Whatever has gotten into you, I'm not buying it. Take me back to town!"

He just looked happier.

Five miles later she said in a hushed voice, because she was getting scared, "Are you kidnapping me?"

"Sort of." His smile widened.

When they took the Greenwich exit she sank her head into her hands. "Greenwich," she moaned. "Max, I can't afford to live in a toolshed in Greenwich. What is this? What are you doing? I want to go home. Well, I can't go home, but I want to go...somewhere besides here."

She was still moaning when he pulled into a driveway and came to a stop. Warily she separated the fingers over her right eye to peer out. She saw a white clapboard house set well back from the tree-lined street, late-afternoon sunlight dappling the lush green, shaded lawn. She took both hands off her eyes and stared.

The house wasn't huge, just big and comfortable and serene-looking. She was sitting in the driveway in a family car. She could almost hear the children's voices, smell the eggs and bacon she'd cooked for their breakfast, the tuna fish she'd made for the sandwiches in their lunch boxes.

And sitting beside her in the car...

"Like it so far?" Max said.

"This is a joke, a really cruel joke," she said, her heart breaking with longing. "I don't understand. You know I can't buy a house, and certainly not this house, or is it a boarding house and I'm supposed to rent a room?"

"I'll explain. After I bought the car, I decided I needed a house to go with it. I'm not positive this is the one I want, but it's close."

"You're buying a house. How can you afford it?" She practically yelled it at him.

"Well. First of all, my grandfather Laughton wasn't exactly a small-town newspaperman like Dad. When he died, he owned about sixty papers."

Blythe gasped.

"Plus my grandmother McPherson, Mom's mother, inherited a thousand dollars in the fifties and bought a hundred shares of IBM." Over the cry Blythe couldn't keep back, he went on. "That was about seventeen stock-splits ago. Everybody inherited. So that's how I can afford the house and the car and still do the work I love to do."

"I see," Blythe said in a very small voice.

"But you need help with a house like this," he said, "and I'm offering you the job."

A strange lightness began to take over Blythe's body as she sat there, feeling the entire world change around her.

"I'm going to need a decorator and a housekeeper, a cook and a bookkeeper, a gardener, and a chauffeur to take me to the train every weekday morning." He unfastened his seat belt and began edging toward her.

"I'll need a personal shopper, a travel agent, a pet-sitter and someday, a nanny."

He was right beside her now, looking down at her, his beautiful blue eyes serious as they studied her face. "Now this is a lot of work," he said. "There would have to be some additional staff, but this one person would be in charge, so I'm prepared to pay a handsome salary. And the benefits, Blythe—" he lowered his head "—will be out of this world." His mouth found hers and his arms went around her.

Dazed, she simply sank into the kiss and let him hold her. Funny, but it felt like home.

"Want the job?" he said when he finally ended the kiss.

"I want to go over the contract first," she whispered, "and I think a probationary period is in order."

"We don't need one. I already know you can..."

"Not for me," she said. "For you. Then we need to have a serious discussion about my title."

He hugged her so tightly she could hardly breathe. "Let's run through the house and then go home. Together."

Sacha didn't sound a bit surprised when Blythe called to apologize for the fact that she wouldn't be showing up to spend the weekend.

"I WAS SUCH AN IDIOT," Max said the next day. It was Saturday, nearly noon, and he still hadn't said all the things he wanted to say to her. He held her tight, stroking her hair, pressing soft kisses into it. "All the signs that you were exactly the woman I'd been looking for were right there in front of me, but I was too dumb to read them."

"We can't expect you to be as sensitive as Garth,"

she said, squinting one sparkling green eye up at him. Hunger had finally forced them out of bed, into the shower and into enough clothes to go out to lunch.

He took her earlobe in his teeth and nibbled on it. "Ha. Just you wait. You don't know sensitive. I'll make you eat those words." His mouth closed on hers in a kiss he tried to turn into a promise, a promise to give her the home she'd never had, to make her happy forever, to triple the national average for sexual frequency in married couples. He planned to start there, with that last one, and was enthusiastically warming up to resume his awesome obligation to that goal when his cell phone called to him from his jacket pocket.

"Ignore it," he whispered.

"You'd better answer it."

"We already know what happens when we answer the phone. I'm not going to put any phones in our new house."

The phone kept ringing. "Frigging phone," Blythe muttered at last. "Answer it. I'm already completely distracted."

"Language," he growled, gleaped up and snatched it out of his pocket. "Hello." His tone should have scared off the person who dared to call at this crucial minute. But it didn't. He listened. He sat down hard in his Thonet rocker.

Blythe knelt beside him. "What is it, Max? Something bad?"

He rested a shaky hand on her shoulder. "This afternoon?" he asked the caller. "You said *this* afternoon?"

"Oh, Max." From the look on her face he could tell she thought he'd lost a loved one, and he felt that he had, if only for the hours from one to seven.

"I'll be here," he said, pushed the End button and

gazed at Blythe's worried face. Her worried, beautiful, loving, caring little face. He loved her. How could he ever have doubted it? And now he wouldn't be able to show her how much until...

"That was the phone company," he said, being perfectly calm as he felt he always was—well, almost always. "They're coming between one and seven to hook up my phone service."

She just stared back. "On Saturday? Coming now? It *is* one o'clock. They've made you wait a month and they're coming *now* to hook you up, now when you were about to—"

"About to tell you how desperately I love you," he said softly, "about to show you how desperately I love you, about to give you your engagement ring now instead of waiting until dinner and champagne tonight—"

"They've destroyed the most important moment of my life," Blythe said mournfully.

"Aw," he said, poking his lower lip out in a way that made Blythe want to nibble on it. "Well," he added, suddenly brisk, "I know what we can do while we wait. Make lists! We can make a list of everything we have to do to put on the wedding. You can make a list of kitchen staples you'll need when we move into the house. Think of the time it will save then to know exactly what we need on the shelves! Then we can—"

"Are you insane?" Blythe shrieked, and jumped him, landing on his lap with her legs stuck through the arms of the rocker, pinning him against it, the skirt of her sundress riding up until her panties showed. "There are much better ways to use our time while we wait! Like this." She seized his mouth in a demanding, purposeful kiss.

Oh, well, okay, if you insist. He kissed her back. With fervor. His arms slid around her, he pulled her tight against him, he closed his eyes against the hot rush of desire...

And of course, on cue, the phone company arrived.

If they'd been a normal, ordinary couple, the phone company wouldn't have come until just after seven o'clock. But he and Blythe were not, and would never be, an ordinary couple.

Sacha's second book was going to be a blockbuster.

If it didn't get banned in Boston.

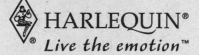

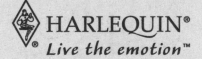

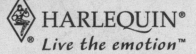